J

A **FRIENDLY TOWN**
THAT'S ALMOST ALWAYS
BY THE OCEAN!

MAR - - - 2019

CH

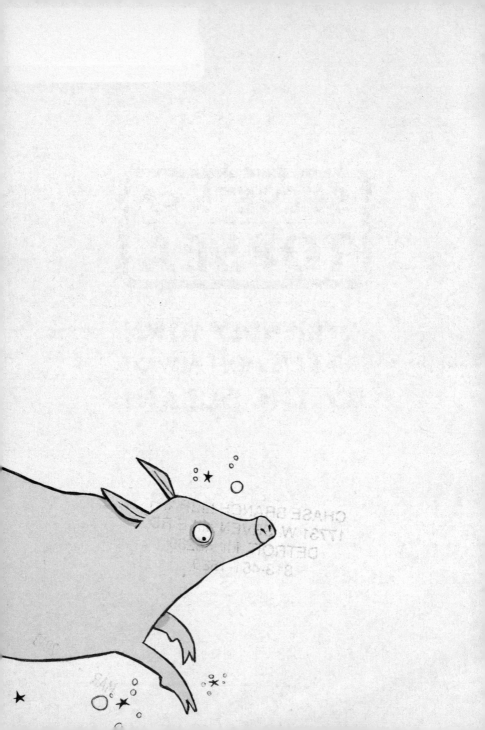

SECRETS of TOPSEA

A FRIENDLY TOWN THAT'S ALMOST ALWAYS BY THE OCEAN!

Kir Fox & M. Shelley Coats

Illustrated by Rachel Sanson

DISNEP • HYPERION

LOS ANGELES   NEW YORK

Text copyright © 2018 by Kirsten Hubbard and Michelle Schusterman
Illustrations copyright © 2018 by Rachel Sanson

First Hardcover Edition, April 2018
First Paperback Edition, January 2019
1 3 5 7 9 10 8 6 4 2
FAC-025438-18327
Printed in the United States of America

This book is set in 12.25-pt Bodoni LT Pro/Monotype, Adobe Devanagari/Fontspring; Bodoni Svntytwo ITC Pro, Goudy Modern MT Pro, ITC Franklin Gothic Std, Fournier MT Pro/Monotype
Designed by Maria Elias

Library of Congress Cataloging-in-Publication Control Number for Hardcover Edition: 201703664
ISBN 978-1-368-00080-2

Visit www.DisneyBooks.com

SUSTAINABLE FORESTRY INITIATIVE
Certified Chain of Custody
Promoting Sustainable Forestry
www.sfiprogram.org
SFI-01054
The SFI label applies to the text stock

To the kids who smile with all of their teeth

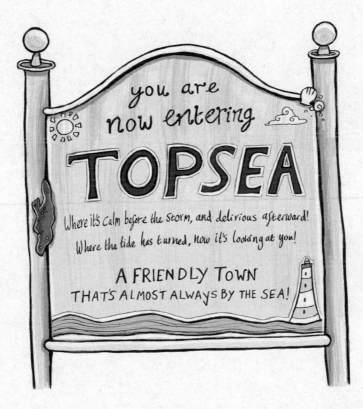

From

EVERYTHING YOU NEED TO KNOW ABOUT TOPSEA

by Fox & Coats

Seaweed Season

There are five seasons in the town of Topsea.

The usual ones: Winter, Summer, Autumn, Spring.

And one unusual one: Seaweed Season.

Seaweed Season can arrive anytime. But always after High Tide.

Everybody in Topsea agrees it's the most annoying season. More annoying than summer, when the whole town stinks of rotten fish. More annoying than winter, with the sea fog and that stubborn single hurricane.

More treacherous, too.

During Seaweed Season, seaweed winds through the spokes

1

of your bike tires. It wraps around your mailbox. It clings to your ankles.

Sometimes on purpose.

It wriggles in through the drains of your bathtub and kitchen sink. Worst of all, a few pieces always end up in bed with you. Under your sheets. Twisting around your toes right when you start to fall asleep.

The cafeteria workers try to make the best of Seaweed Season. But a kid can only eat so many seaweed burgers. On seaweed buns. With seaweed ketchup.

There's one good thing about Seaweed Season: it's short. When High Tide returns, the seaweed is gone.

Make sure you check under your sheets tonight, though.

Just in case.

Davy

1.

Davy's First Day

Davy Jones was distressed about the location of his locker.

Maybe he was making too big a deal of it. After all, his nerves were kind of frazzled. His first day of fifth grade at Topsea School had gotten off to a bumpy start. He'd flattened his bike tire on a speed bump and ended up walking most of the way.

The walk had been a little strange, too. Because Topsea was a little strange. At least, it was to Davy. But he'd never lived on the coast before.

According to his mom, they'd get used to the oddities. Like how the lighthouse sat in the middle of town, far from the water.

It was painted red and white with a lantern room at the top. It had no doors or ladders or stairs. But a lighthouse keeper lived up there, swooping light across the town every night. She'd waved at Davy through the lantern room window that morning.

Then there was the long stretch of rocks by the beach, covered with more cats than Davy could count. They stared at him with yellow eyes whenever he passed by.

And then there was the pier, which just kept going and going out into the ocean until it disappeared into the horizon.

Not to mention the schoolyard, which was all sand and dead grass that crunched beneath Davy's feet. On the playground, the slides and swings appeared normal enough, but the jungle gym looked a whole lot like a pirate ship's masts sticking out of the ground.

"Just a part of coastal life," Davy muttered to himself.

That's what his mom had said earlier that morning, when their mail had been delivered by a seagull instead of a mailperson.

"Things are just a little different here," she'd continued, watching through the kitchen window as the bird rammed its beak into their mailbox. "When I worked at the cheese shop back home, I didn't have to worry about cheese hiding in my shoes. Topsea's seaweed cracker factory is another story."

"But it's not *normal*," Davy had insisted. "Even this house is weird. The basement door is sealed shut. The wallpaper smells like fish. And it's so *small*."

His mom had given him a tired sort of smile, unwinding a stubborn strand of seaweed from her shoelaces. "Don't worry, Davy. We'll both adjust. We just have to try."

Davy had nodded.

He wanted life to go back to normal. He wanted his old town with his old house and no seaweed in sight.

Most of all, he wanted his dad back.

Of course, that was impossible. Davy's mom was right. Nothing was normal anymore, and it never would be again. He just needed to adjust.

But this whole locker thing was just plain *weird*.

"It's at the bottom of the swimming pool?" Davy asked, clutching his schedule.

Mr. Zapple, the school counselor, nodded patiently. "Of course," he said. "In the deep end. You'll find everything you need to know about Topsea down there!"

"*Everything* I need to know?"

"Along with all your textbooks, safe as can be."

"But why?" Davy sputtered. "Why just *my* locker? Is it because I'm new?"

"Exactly!" Mr. Zapple smiled, making his extra-large ears stick out even more. "It's our most prized locker. We wanted to make you feel welcome."

Davy blinked several times. "But how do I—"

"Oh, I almost forgot." The counselor pushed aside a copy of *The Topsea School Gazette*, then handed Davy a piece of paper. "This is a mandatory new student survey, just for my records. Feel free to take your time with it, okay?"

"Okay, but . . . but my locker . . ."

The bell rang. Mr. Zapple patted Davy's arm. "Don't worry, Dexter. I know starting a new school is scary, but you'll be just fine!"

"It's Davy," said Davy.

He hurried down a hall with rows of red lockers. Another hall with rows of yellow lockers. He passed dozens of students, all twirling combination locks and slamming locker doors without even having to hold their breath.

At last, Davy reached the gym, where he found an Olympic-size indoor swimming pool. The kindergarten class played mermaid tag in the shallow end. Their teacher watched from a lifeguard chair. Davy walked past them to the deep end.

It was very, very deep.

Squinting, Davy spotted a small, gray rectangle at the bottom of the pool, directly beneath the diving board. He swallowed hard.

Being the new kid in school takes a lot of courage sometimes. Apparently, this was one of those times.

Davy set down his empty backpack, wishing he'd brought his swim trunks. He kicked off his tennis shoes and climbed the ladder to the diving board. He walked to the edge and looked down.

His locker was a shimmering gray dot.

Davy didn't know how to dive. He was much better at land sports, like skeeball.

But his dad *had* taught him how to do cannonballs.

So Davy sucked in a giant breath and cannonballed off the diving board. The splash was huge! All the kindergartners clapped and flapped their mermaid tails in appreciation. Davy didn't hear them, since he was already several feet underwater.

He opened his eyes, saw the gray locker, and kicked hard. He swam deeper and deeper, but his locker was still just a dot.

Finally, Davy gave up. He broke the surface of the pool right as the tardy bell rang. He climbed out, shaking the water from his shaggy, brown hair. How could he ever swim that deep? And even if he did, how was he supposed to get his books to the surface without ruining them?

And why did everyone act like this was all *normal*?

As Davy passed the kindergartners in the shallow end, they clapped and flapped again. "That was a wonderful cannonball," their teacher told him.

"Thanks," Davy said. "I'm pretty good at dog-paddling, too."

The kindergartners giggled.

Davy drip-dropped all the way to class. Outside the door, he sucked in a huge breath like he was about to cannonball. Then he stepped inside.

"Was it High Tide this morning?" his new teacher asked. She had stripy-looking gray hair and wore tortoiseshell glasses.

"Uh, no," Davy began. "I'm sorry I'm late. You see, my locker is at the bottom of the pool, and . . ."

Then he realized the teacher's question hadn't been for him. In fact, she hadn't even heard him. She was talking to a girl with a long, brown braid sitting near the window.

"No, there was no High Tide this morning," the girl said.

"And how can you tell, Nia?"

Nia pointed dramatically out the window. "Because there was no morning moon!"

"Very good." Finally, the teacher noticed Davy standing in a giant puddle by the door. "Well, it looks like our new student is here!"

Smiling, she beckoned Davy over to her desk. Her nails were very pointy.

"We were just starting our lesson on meteorology," she said. "I'm Ms. Grimalkin, by the way."

"I'm sorry I'm late, Ms. Grimalkin," Davy said nervously. "I couldn't get to my locker, and now I'm soaking wet."

"I understand. It's easy to get soaked on your first day at a new school. What's your name?"

"Davy Jones."

Ms. Grimalkin peered at her roll sheet. "Ah, there you are!" She wrote a little check. Then she pointed to a desk beside a boy with dark skin and red wire-rimmed glasses. "You can sit next to Quincy, Daniel."

"It's Davy," said Davy. "Um. Do you have a towel I could use?"

"Sorry," Ms. Grimalkin said sympathetically. "But I'm sure there's one in your locker."

Davy opened his mouth. Maybe to ask why his locker was in the pool. Maybe to explain that he couldn't dive that deep. Maybe to point out that even if he could, by the time he surfaced with the towel, it would be soaked, too.

Then he remembered he was supposed to be adjusting.

So he closed his mouth and drip-dropped over to his desk and sat down next to Quincy, who smiled at him. In fact, everyone was smiling at him. All of them at once. Davy pushed his wet hair out of his eyes, feeling self-conscious.

"I like your shirt," Nia said. "It's just like the legend!"

Davy glanced down at his soaked shirt. It was blue and had a picture of a dog howling at the moon. "Oh," he said. "Thank you. What legend?"

"AROOOO!" Nia howled, and the class giggled.

Davy tried to smile. Even though he couldn't tell if this was the kind of laughter that was *with* you or *at* you. But the other kids seemed nice. Especially Quincy, who shared his textbooks with Davy for the rest of the lesson.

In fact, things seemed almost normal.

Then came lunchtime.

Davy stood between Quincy and Nia in the hot-lunch line. A burly man in a hairnet scooped out french fries. A tattoo of a fork and a butter knife in an X shape decorated his left bicep. His name tag said *Ricky*.

"Fries or clams?" Ricky asked Davy, pointing to two pans. One pan was piled high with brown-and-gray clams. Some of them seemed to peek out of their shells at Davy. The other pan was empty.

Chewing his lip, Davy glanced at the clams again. Their shells slammed shut. "Um . . . fries?" he said.

"Okay, just a minute." Ricky turned and bellowed, "Potato hunt! Where's the spudzooka?"

"Right here!" a cafeteria woman called. She had thick, strong arms and a tiny spatula earring in her left ear. Her name tag said *Nicky*. She grabbed what looked like a miniature cannon off the wall and heaved it at Ricky.

Ricky caught the spudzooka with one hand. He pushed through the double doors to the kitchen, where Davy saw two more cafeteria workers waving a red cape in front of the ovens. He caught a glimpse of a buffalo charging them just before the doors swung closed.

"Why is there a buffalo in the kitchen?" Davy asked, alarmed.

Nia laughed. "Because tomorrow is hamburger day!"

Davy opened his mouth. Maybe to say that normal school cafeterias didn't include wild animals. Maybe to point out that hamburger meat usually came from cows. Maybe to add that cows in a school cafeteria would also be really weird.

Then he remembered again. He was supposed to *adjust*.

So he closed his mouth. But he was starting to wish he'd brought a packed lunch. His dad used to make the funniest sandwiches, like pickle and peanut butter or ham and apricot jelly. They were kind of gross, but also kind of good, once you got used to the taste.

Ricky returned a minute later, sweaty and holding a pan filled with piping-hot french fries. He piled a handful on a plate for Davy. They had just the right amount of salt, although they tasted a bit like clams.

"We have real ketchup today, thank goodness," Quincy said, dousing his french fries.

Nia nodded in agreement. "Seaweed ketchup just isn't the same."

Davy had never tasted seaweed ketchup. But last week, his mom had brought home a whole sack of seaweed crackers that had been overpeppered. Davy didn't like them very much. They were far chewier than crackers should be. And sometimes they seemed to chew you back.

"You look kind of pale, Danny," Quincy observed.

Nia gasped loudly. "Do you have food poisoning? Do you have the flu? Are you contagious?"

"No!" Davy said, although his stomach felt all twisty-turny. "I'm not sick. Please pass the ketchup."

Quincy handed him the bottle. Davy focused on smothering his fries in ketchup, and soon Quincy and Nia were busy discussing the local water park, Hanger Cliffs, which was supposed to reopen soon. Davy *loved* water parks, and before long he forgot all about charging buffalos and peeking clams.

Back in the classroom, Ms. Grimalkin started a lesson on animals.

"All animals have special characteristics that make them different from other animals," Ms. Grimalkin said. "For example, seagulls have long bills just perfect for stuffing letters in mailboxes."

She pointed to a quiet girl with shiny pigtails and brown skin. "Talise, can you name two characteristics of fish?"

"What particular species of fish?" Talise asked.

"Fish in general," Ms. Grimalkin said.

Talise cleared her throat. "Well, the majority have scales and breathe through gills. Some can use camouflage to hide from predators. All lack vocal cords, but many make sounds by vibrating their other muscles. They— "

"Thank you, Talise," Ms. Grimalkin interrupted. "Let's give someone else a turn. What about pigs?"

Nia's hand shot up. "They have curly tails and dig with their snouts!"

"Very good. And cats?" Ms. Grimalkin asked, looking around with an extra-wide smile. "Finn, can you answer this one? Speak up."

Finn, a tiny, pale boy with auburn hair, nodded nervously. "They have sharp claws," he said. At least, that's what Davy thought he said. Finn's voice was even smaller than he was.

"And you can see all of their teeth when they smile!" added the pretty girl sitting beside Finn. She had choppy black hair and light skin. Her shirt appeared to be covered in colorful paint.

"Excellent, Runa," Ms. Grimalkin purred. "What other animal characteristics can we think of?"

Davy glanced at Quincy, who was busy scribbling in a note-book. He was feeling better now. He'd had a nice lunch and his clothes were almost dry. So he put his hand in the air.

"Yes?" Ms. Grimalkin said.

"Dogs are good hunters," Davy announced. "And they wag their tails when they're happy."

"AROOOO!" the class cried before bursting into giggles.

Davy smiled, but he felt like he'd missed a joke somewhere.

Ms. Grimalkin smiled, too. "You're very funny," she said. "I'm glad you're in this class, Darwin."

"It's Davy," Davy said with a sigh.

After school, Davy walked back to his new home with the sealed-up basement door and wallpaper that smelled like fish. He tried to figure out whether his first day at school had been good or bad, since he knew his mom would ask. Today definitely hadn't been *normal*. But that didn't mean it was a *bad* day, right? After all, weird could be good once you got used to it, like a pickle-and-peanut-butter sandwich.

Topsea was more like a crab-and-seaweed-ketchup sandwich, though. The kind of weird Davy didn't want to get used to.

As Davy passed the rock cats, the tide suddenly rushed in.

"Ack!" he exclaimed.

Davy frowned at his soaked shoes and pants. A strand of sea-weed clung to his shoelaces. "I never figured out how to get to my locker," he realized.

The rock cats smiled at him. Davy could see all of their teeth.

From

EVERYTHING YOU NEED TO KNOW ABOUT TOPSEA

by Fox & Coats

The Legend of the Dogs

As transcribed from the hieroglyphics in the Untold Caves

Centuries ago, before Topsea was a town, mermaids ruled over the coast.

They lived on the rocks where the land and sea met, braiding seaweed into their hair and watching the sky for signs.

Especially signs of treachery and betrayal.

The mermaids were deeply mistrustful by nature. But they were fond of the dogs that lived near the water, paddling during High Tide and frolicking during Low Tide. The dogs fetched seaweed and performed tricks. The mermaids rewarded them by clapping and flapping their fins.

The dogs loved the mermaids. After all, mermaids are half
human.

The cats watched, too. They lived on the sandy banks, sharp-
ening their claws on the rocks and catching crabs that scuttled
too far from the water.

The cats loved the mermaids. After all, mermaids are half
fish.

One night, the mermaids read a warning in the stars. An
enemy was plotting to take the rocks, banishing the mermaids
from the coast and sending them to the depths of the ocean.

But who was the enemy?

The mermaids had noticed the hungry way the cats eyed the rocks. And so they confronted the cats first.

"Banish you out to sea?" the cats replied. "Heavens no. If anything, we'd like you to come closer. And what could we possibly want with the rocks?"

The mermaids considered this.

"If you ask us," the cats continued, "it is the dogs who wish to take the rocks. They grow tired of performing tricks for you."

The mermaids looked at one another. It was true, the dogs were very good at performing tricks. They really were very tricky. The dogs would probably rather rest on the rocks than perform trick after trick in the water.

The dogs, the mermaids realized with horror, were the real enemy.

So the mermaids devised a plan. They waited until a night when the moon was nowhere to be seen. Then they unwound the seaweed from their hair, leaped into the water, and challenged the dogs to a game of tug-of-war.

The dogs happily agreed to play. The cats ventured out onto the rocks to watch the game. As the mermaids tugged and tugged and the dogs wagged and wagged, the tide began to retreat. The mermaids and dogs drifted farther out to sea until they were mere specks in the distance. As the sun began to rise, the mermaids let go of the seaweed. The tide vanished beyond the horizon.

So did the dogs.

The mermaids returned to the rocks, where they found their

cat friends waiting. Exhausted, the mermaids fell asleep as the cats' smiles grew wider and wider and wider. . . .

The dogs were never seen again. But on moonless nights, their distant howls can be heard from the rocks. *AROOOOO!*

Authors' note: Much like dinosaurs or dodo birds, scientists don't know exactly how or why mermaids went extinct. All we know for sure is that they definitely existed.

Unlike dogs, which are, of course, just a myth.

THE TOPSEA SCHOOL GAZETTE

Today's Tide: Low

WORD OF THE DAY

Sesquipedalian (n.): A really long word.

FEELING CRABBY?

by Jules, Fifth-Grade Star Reporter

As many students have probably noticed, this morning the beach was covered in a large cast of black crabs after last night's unexpected Severely Low Tide.

These crabs range in size from "pea" to "soccer ball," and the largest ones appear to have triple-jointed legs. The new crabs have scared off the regular pink crabs, who have gone into hiding in the basement of Lost Soles shoe store. The owner, Miss Meiko, is celebrating her store's new inhabitants with a buy-one, get-one-half-off sale on all footwear. But take a tip from this reporter, who tried on a cute pair of sneakers during her investigation: check the inside of the shoe before you stick your foot in it, or you just might lose a toe!

As for the new black crabs, not much else is known about them. They scuttle extra fast, making them almost impossible to catch. When the tide came in late this morning, witnesses reported seeing them stack on top of one another to form pyramids on the driftwood. One witness thought it looked like the crabs were trying to avoid getting wet. This reporter finds their behavior highly suspicious, as crabs usually love water, and will report more as the situation develops.

PEARLS OF WISDOM

by Miss J, Totally Anonymous Advice Columnist

Dear Miss J,

My family is really big and REALLY loud. I'm the youngest and the quietest. My friends talk over me a lot, too. Sometimes I feel like I'm invisible! How can I get everyone to pay attention to me?

Sincerely,

A Mouse

Dear Mouse,

You should do something BIG to get your family and friends' attention! Try dyeing your hair pink, or wearing extra-loud clompy boots, or using a megaphone when you talk. Ignoring someone is extremely rude, and your friends and family should know better. Good luck!

Miss J

ALERT: Several gallons of milk have gone missing from the cafeteria. If you have any information, please contact Nicky or Ricky in the cafeteria.

2.

Earl Grey

A ray of sunlight shone weakly through the fog. The clotted seaweed by the seashore stank less than yesterday. Nia's nanny wasn't making fish loaf for supper.

Those were all reasons to be excited. But not Nia's reason.

"He's coming today!" she told the seagulls on her way to school.

"He's coming today!" she told her classmates, Ms. Grimalkin, and Mr. Zapple with his mouth full of Indian food from the new deli.

"Today!" she told the rock cats on her way home. They stared back at her with yellow eyes.

The seagulls typically made big postal deliveries around noon. But as Nia sprinted up the driveway to her house, she discovered the porch was empty. Her heart broke into a thousand million pieces. (That's how it felt to Nia, anyway.)

She threw open the double front doors. "Nannyyyy!" she cried. "Where *is* he?"

"He's in your room, mija," her nanny called from the living room, where she was watching her three o'clock telenovela.

"Thank you!"

Nia ran up her family's spiral staircase and into her room. A small wooden crate sat in the middle of her bed. It had holes punched in the lid and DO NOT SHAKE painted on the side.

The crate shook.

Nia shrieked, jumping up and down. Then she undid the latch. The tiniest pig she'd ever seen somersaulted out. He was light pink with gray spots. Nia kissed him on the end of his snout, then grabbed a teacup from her tea party set and held him up to compare.

"Almost exactly the same size," she said.

"Snort," said the pig.

"I think I'll call you Earl Grey."

"Snuffle," said Earl Grey.

Nia had wanted a teacup pig as long as she could remember. Usually, her mom and dad bought her whatever she wanted, but that was mostly stuff like dresses and sports equipment and fancy cameras. A real, live pig was another story.

"*¿Un puerco?*" her mom always said, wrinkling her nose, while her dad made jokes about carnitas and bacon.

But lately, the family's international real estate business had grown more successful, and they'd been traveling to Mexico City much more often. "I *need* a companion!" Nia had begged them in her most dramatic fashion. "*Desperately*. Nanny spends all her time watching telenovelas. And I can't fit her in my pocket, even if I wanted to."

At long last, Nia had managed to convince them.

And now her dream had come true!

She beamed at Earl Grey. He smiled back. Nia took one of her hair ribbons and tied it onto his curly tail, then stuffed him inside the teacup and took a picture with her fancy camera.

For breakfast, she fed Earl Grey a big bowl of oatmeal, as per the instructions in *The Care and Training of Teacup Pigs*. When he was finished, she slipped a collar over his head, then walked him to school on a leash. The rock cats stared hungrily as she passed.

"Don't even think about it," Nia told them.

At school, everybody crowded around Nia and her new pet. "This is Earl Grey," she said proudly. "He's a purebred teacup pig!"

"*Aww*," Quincy said. "What a cute little piggie."

"Are you sure he's a pig?" Jules asked, flipping back her blond curls. "He looks like a hamster."

Earl Grey snorted indignantly.

"He's definitely a teacup pig!" Nia said. "I checked. And besides, I ordered him from a breeder on the Internet."

"You mean, your *parents* ordered him," Jules said.

Nia rolled her eyes. Jules, the class reporter, was Nia's best friend. She was also Nia's greatest rival. That meant they bickered constantly—but if anyone else tried to bicker with Jules, they had Nia to answer to. And the other way around.

"You're so lucky," Finn said. "My parents only order takeout food."

"He can sit right here, if you like," Ms. Grimalkin said, tapping her sharp, pointy nails on Nia's desk. "He's so adorable. I could just eat him up!"

Earl Grey sat on Nia's desk all through class. He paid attention to every one of Ms. Grimalkin's lessons, which made Nia feel even prouder.

At lunchtime, the cafeteria workers brought Earl Grey a bowl of oatmeal. They all stuck around to watch him eat. "We had to make it with water," said Ricky, his burly arms crossed over his barrel chest. "Somebody's been stealing our milk."

"That's okay," Nia said as Earl Grey dove into the bowl face-first. "He seems to like it just fine."

"He's the cutest pig I've ever seen," said Nicky, patting Earl Grey's head. "And the hungriest!"

That night, Earl Grey curled up at the foot of Nia's bed. Her heart glowed with the warmth of a thousand suns. (That's how it felt to Nia, anyway.)

The next morning, she fed him a fresh bowl of oatmeal. Then she tried to stuff him inside the teacup again. But for some reason, he wouldn't fit. In fact, he appeared to have tripled in size overnight.

"Too much oatmeal!" Nia scolded. "Then again, I suppose if anyone's allowed to eat like a pig, it's a pig."

"Snuffle," replied Earl Grey.

Nia put the teacup on Earl Grey's head and took a picture.

At school, Earl Grey sat on Nia's desk again. But now she had to lean to the side to see around him.

"Is it normal for pigs to grow that fast?" asked Davy. "Earl Grey looks a lot bigger."

"You're seeing things, Damian," Nia said. But she wondered.

At lunch, they learned the milk truck hadn't even made it to school that day. "Something popped every single one of its tires," Ricky said grouchily. "Something real sharp."

But she cheered up as they all watched Earl Grey eat. The pig gobbled up his oatmeal so quickly, Nicky brought him a second bowl, then a third.

"Snort!" Earl Grey said happily, spraying oatmeal everywhere.

"Hmm," Nia said.

The morning after that, the teacup wouldn't even fit on Earl Grey's head. Nia removed the teacup and scowled at it. "What else is this thing good for?"

She used one of her ribbons to tie the teacup to Earl Grey's curly tail. She got out her camera, then shook her head and put it away.

As Nia and Earl Grey walked to school, Finn and Runa caught up with them. "Did you ever hear about the time there was a blizzard way up in the mountains?" Runa asked Nia. "And a snowball started rolling down the hill, and it got bigger and bigger and bigger? Until it rolled right into town and exploded into a million billion snowflakes?"

"Suuuuure," Nia said.

Everybody knew Runa's stories were mostly make-believe. But still, Nia couldn't help picturing Earl Grey rolling down a hill, getting bigger and bigger and bigger, until . . .

"Pop," she said.

Beside her, Earl Grey let out an apprehensive snuffle.

When they entered the classroom, Earl Grey tried to sit on Nia's desk as usual. The desk creaked and groaned under his weight.

"What is that?" Jules asked. "It sounds like a dying seagull."

"I don't hear anything," Nia lied.

Suddenly Nia's desk broke, falling to the ground with a deafening crash. Earl Grey was sent tumbling tail over snout. "Oink! Oink!" he squealed.

"Oh no!" Nia exclaimed. She tried to pick him up, but he was too big. She patted him on the head to make him feel better.

Ms. Grimalkin called in Cosmo the janitor to fix Nia's desk. When he saw Earl Grey, he raised his eyebrows. "What's that you've got there?"

"He's my teacup pig," Nia said. "His name's Earl Grey."

"Are you sure?"

Nia nodded. "I'm the one who named him."

"I mean, are you sure he's a teacup pig?"

"Well, he's definitely not a hamster."

Cosmo scratched his beard. "He doesn't look teacup-size, is all. In fact, he looks an awful lot like a watch hog."

Nia's heart began to flip-flop. "A watch hog?" she repeated.

"A purebred watch hog, I'd say."

"Uh-oh," Ms. Grimalkin said. "Watch hogs aren't allowed in the classroom. The PTA President sent out a notification last week."

Nia groaned. The PTA President had rules for *everything*. "Could you double-check for me, please?"

Ms. Grimalkin pulled out a thick binder and flipped through it. "Let's see. *Walruses*, *Warthogs*, *Wasps* . . . Ah, there it is: *Watch Hogs*. I'm sorry, Nia. Earl Grey will have to wait outside."

"Okay," Nia said.

An ocean of tears pressed behind her eyes. (That's how it felt to Nia, anyway.) She tied Earl Grey's leash to her desk and strung it out the window, where the watch hog waited patiently on the crunchy, shell-strewn grass. Every time Nia glanced outside, he looked bigger.

Nia bit her fingernails. She would call the breeder when she got home, she decided, and give him a piece of her mind. Nia liked Earl Grey, but she hadn't always wanted a watch hog. She'd wanted a teacup pig.

All of a sudden there was a high-pitched wailing outside.

HWEEE! HWEEE! HWEEE!

"Oh dear," Quincy said worriedly. "I think that's the fire alarm. Ms. Grimalkin, should I go find a hose?"

"No way!" Jules said. "It sounds like the hurricane siren. Ms. Grimalkin, should we grab our umbrellas?"

Then came a hissing and spitting sound. The wailing grew even louder. But it didn't quite sound like a siren, or even an alarm. In fact, it sounded an awful lot like . . . *a pig.*

Nia ran to the window to look.

Earl Grey had a rock cat by the tail! Rock cats almost never visited the schoolyard—and this cat was the angriest one Nia had ever seen. It twisted and flailed, trying to claw Earl Grey, but its paws couldn't reach. Earl Grey squealed and squealed. The cat yowled and yowled.

All the other kids crowded behind Nia.

"Wow!" exclaimed Runa. "Your pig is super brave."

Even Jules looked impressed. "Yeah, those rock cats are awfully mean."

"Really?" Davy asked. "They smile more than the cats I'm used to."

"That's because they're always up to something," Finn said, but his tiny voice was drowned out by a pathetic cry from outside.

"MROOOW," the rock cat wailed.

"Oh, sorry," Nia said. "Earl Grey! You can put it down now!"

Earl Grey released the rock cat. It darted away, wailing at the top of its lungs. Several other rock cats followed, leaping across the schoolyard toward the sea.

At lunch, the cafeteria workers made Earl Grey an extra-large helping of oatmeal, served in their biggest mixing bowl. It was more delicious than usual, since it was made with hot milk instead of water.

"Turns out the rock cats were getting into the milk," said Nicky. "Although someone must've unlocked the back door to let them in . . ."

"Rumor has it your teacup pig is the one who squealed?" asked Ricky.

"Yep!" Nia said proudly. "Except he's not a teacup pig. He's a purebred watch hog."

Earl Grey smiled up at Nia, dripping oatmeal all over her shoes.

Nia smiled back at him, her heart so filled with love the entire solar system was playing pinball inside her chest, zinging and zapping and sparkling with comets and meteors and supernovas. (That's how it felt to Nia, anyway.)

(And to Earl Grey, too.)

NOTIFICATION: TOWN TIDE ALERTS

Courtesy of the Town Committee for Lunar Phase Observance and Moontime Celebration

LOW TIDE

Water level: Pretty low.

Ideal for: Fishing, clam digging, and sunbathing.

SEVERELY LOW TIDE

Water level: Distant line on the horizon.

Ideal for: Sand-castle building, tide-pool exploring, and collecting shells and teeth.

WARNING: Do not attempt to walk all the way out to the water. If you can't see the bluffs, you've gone out too far. Turn back immediately.

VANISHING TIDE

Water level: Nonexistent.

Ideal for: Bathymetry research, swimming lessons for aquaphobes.

SPECIAL NOTE: Avoid collecting seaweed during Vanishing Tide, as they feel very exposed and would like some privacy.

HIGH TIDE

Water level: Pretty high.

Ideal for: Surfing, snorkeling, and scuba diving.

EXTREMELY HIGH TIDE

Water level: May reach town center.

Ideal for: Street surfing and extreme synchronized swimming (license required).

WARNING: Seal your windows and doors. Galoshes are recommended. Be sure nonamphibious pets, such as gerbils and watch hogs, have access to flotation devices.

WILDCARD TIDE

Any of the aforementioned tides may occur at any time. Twice as fun as Hanger Cliffs Water Park, and half as deadly!

NOTIFICATION: WATER PARK FLYER

NEW STUDENT SURVEY

by Davy Jones

1. Why did you move to Topsea?
My mom made me.

2. What are you most excited to learn about at Topsea School, and why?
I like math, because it makes sense. But the way Ms. Grimalkin teaches it is weird. When she runs out of chalk, she solves problems by scratching them on the wall.

3. What's your biggest fear?
Getting attacked by those rock cats. They give me the CREEPS!

4. What's your favorite hobby?
Fishing.

5. What's your favorite flavor of ice cream?
Pistachio.

6. Do you have any other thoughts you'd like to share?
Mostly, I'm just confused.

Like, how do I KNOW when the tides will change?

What exactly IS a bathymetrist? Talise explained three times and I still don't get it. (And I can never remember how to pronounce it.)

Most of all, what's the deal with those rock cats? They're just not NORMAL!

But that's the thing. Almost nothing about Topsea is normal. Not even you, Mr. Zapple. (No offense. But a locker at the bottom of the swimming pool? Really???)

I know my mom really wants me to like it here, and I don't want to let her down. This year's been really hard for both of us. And I know I haven't been in Topsea very long at all.

But it's nothing like my hometown. The school is nothing like my school back home. The kids are nothing like my friends back home. . . .

~~Maybe I'm more homesick than I thought.~~

Davy

3.

A Tour of Town

"It's so nice out this morning," Davy's mom said, adding cracked pepper to her crab-and-cheese omelet. "You should spend the day outside. Do something fun."

Davy picked at his eggs. "Like what?"

"Like anything! My supervisor at the seaweed cracker factory mentioned there's a great water park in town. You could—"

"It's closed," Davy interrupted. "Quincy told me. They don't know when it'll be open again."

"That's too bad." His mom took a sip of coffee. Then her face brightened. "But who needs a water park when you have the whole ocean? You should go to the beach! Maybe take your fishing pole?"

Davy stared down at his plate. "I don't want . . ." he began, then stopped.

The truth was, he didn't want to go fishing without his dad. But saying so would just make Mom feel bad, and he *really* didn't want to do that. So he forced himself to smile.

"I'm not sure which box I packed it in," he said. "But I can still go to the beach. It'll be fun!"

His mom beamed at him. "Great! I just know we're both going to love it here, Davy."

Davy nodded. But he doubted it.

After breakfast, Davy headed down to the beach. When the grass turned to sand, he kicked off his shoes and carried them, watching for clamshells and stepping over driftwood. He was scrambling over a particularly large and twisty log when he heard a familiar voice.

"Stay! *Stay!* Oh, why won't you stay?"

Davy glanced around until he spotted Nia. She was calling commands to Earl Grey as he snuffled around, blissfully unaware. A few feet away, Jules was perched on a rock beside Quincy, who was scribbling in his notebook. And much farther down the beach, Davy saw Talise crouched in the sand, studying something with a magnifying glass.

"Roll over!" Nia was saying. "Roll *over!*"

"You're not saying it right," Jules told her.

"How would you know?" Nia replied huffily. "You've never trained a watch hog!"

Davy stood uncertainly by the twisty driftwood. Should he go join them? Before he could decide what to do, Quincy glanced up and beamed.

"Daley!" he called, waving. "Hi!"

Somewhat encouraged, Davy walked over to them. "Hi," he said. "It's Davy, actually. With a *v*."

"Do you have any watch-hog training experience?" Jules asked him. "Because Nia could really use an expert."

"I'm doing just fine, thank you," Nia said irritably. She picked up a stick and tossed it toward the water. "Fetch!"

Earl Grey gazed out at the ocean, then back at Nia. He wagged his tail. Nia sighed.

"Are you trying to train him like a dog?" Davy asked.

"A dog?" Nia repeated, looking offended. "Earl Grey might not be easy to train, but he's *real*."

Jules hopped off the log. She smiled at Davy. "How do you like Topsea so far?"

"Oh! It's . . . um . . . ." Davy hesitated. "Nice." *Weird* was what he meant, but he didn't want to offend his new friends. If they actually counted as friends. They were very nice to him, but couldn't seem to remember his name.

"What was your old town like?" Quincy asked.

Davy broke into a grin. "It was great! We lived by a big lake. And there was a really good library, and Main Street had lots of fun places like a comic book store and a movie theater and . . ."

He trailed off. Talking about his old life was making his throat feel funny. Besides, he knew he shouldn't be talking about it at all. He was supposed to be adjusting.

"It doesn't matter," Davy heard himself say. "I don't live there anymore."

"That's true," Nia said. "But I'd still like to hear about it!"

"Me, too," Quincy added. "I've never lived anywhere but Topsea. Moving to a new town sounds kind of scary."

Davy ducked his head. "I'll tell you more about it some other time. It's just . . . different here."

"That's exactly what my stepsister said when she moved away for college," Jules said. "But she loves it there now."

"Really?" Davy said. Jules nodded.

"Why don't we show you around town?" Quincy said eagerly.

"Okay," Davy said. "Um, thanks."

Jules whipped out a notepad and pen. "All right, Davis," she announced. "First stop on your grand tour of Topsea: the beach!"

Davy looked around. "Yeah, I've seen it."

"Not all of it," Jules said. "Follow me!"

She led the way down the beach toward Talise. Quincy and Davy kept up on either side. Nia trailed behind, barking commands at Earl Grey.

"Walk!" she said. *"Heel! Heel! Ow, not* my *heel!"*

Jules turned around and walked backward. "That's just pathetic," she informed Nia. "Isn't there a training book you can buy or something?"

"Well, I *had* a book, but it was for teacup pigs," Nia said crossly.

Davy noticed the rocks in the distance. "Are we going to visit the cats?" he asked nervously. "Because I've already seen them, too."

"But I bet you haven't seen the new crabs yet," Jules said. "They migrated in yesterday. I'm investigating them for the school paper. My stepsister's been giving me tips. She's a journalism major and the best reporter on her college's newspaper staff and—"

"We know, we know," Nia groaned.

"Jules is a great reporter," Quincy told Davy. "And Talise is a great bathymetrist. Do you have a hobby?"

Davy thought about this. "Fishing, I guess. My dad and I used to go fishing at the dock all the time."

"Oh, look!" Nia cried. "Talise just caught one!"

She pointed to Talise, who was surrounded by what looked like a large patch of black sand. But it wasn't sand, Davy realized, stopping short. It was actually a swarm of crabs.

"I should've brought my camera," Nia said with a sigh.

Talise straightened up, crab in one hand and magnifying glass in the other. A tiny claw reached up and swiped at one of her shiny pigtails.

"It's a baby," Talise said as the other kids crowded around her, stepping carefully around the scuttling crabs. "At least, I believe so. These crabs are quite unusual looking."

"I'm glad I'm not the only one who thinks so," Davy said, feeling relieved. "That thumbprint marking on its back can't be normal."

"It sure isn't!" Jules agreed. "That's why I'm investigating them. There's something fishy about these crabs."

Nia rolled her eyes. "They're just crabs, Jules."

"And just because we've never seen them before doesn't mean they're not normal," Talise added. She tapped the baby crab's shell gently, then set it down in the sand with the others.

Davy stepped aside as the crab scuttled off. Talise did have a point, he thought. After all, Davy had never seen a zebra in person. But zebras were normal.

"Well, we should keep going," Jules said, then turned to Talise. "We're showing Declan around town. Wanna come?"

"Thank you, but no. I'd like to keep studying these crabs."

"Let me know if there's any breaking news!" Jules said cheerfully.

"Talise keeps to herself a lot," Quincy told Davy as they walked away. "But when she does come, she's super interesting! So we always ask."

Jules led the group past the rocks and farther down the beach. "We might not have a dock for fishing. But a pier is close enough, right?"

The pier was very, very long. Davy squinted and squinted at the horizon. "Where does it end?" he asked.

Nia laughed. "End? It doesn't end!"

"Normal piers do," Davy insisted. "They're short."

"What's the point of a short pier?" asked Jules. "The ocean is really long."

"Well, you can sit on the end and go fishing," Davy said. "Or cannonball off it, like a diving board."

Nia studied the endless pier. "That *does* sound pretty fun."

"It is," Davy told her. "Back in my old town, I used to cannonball off the dock with my d—"

He closed his mouth abruptly. Jules and Nia gave him a questioning look that he ducked to avoid.

His stomach was doing the twisty-turny thing again. Talking about his old town was one thing. But Davy definitely didn't want to talk about his dad with his classmates. He wasn't sure that his stomach could handle it.

Quincy adjusted his red wire-rimmed glasses. "What else did you do in your old town?"

"Um . . ." Davy chewed his lip. "I went to the library every Saturday."

Jules clapped her hands. "Library! Next stop: town square."

As they headed into town, the other kids chatted happily. Davy didn't join in. He was busy wondering if the endless pier was *really* endless.

Maybe if you walked long enough, you'd find a dad sitting on the edge with two fishing poles, waiting for you.

Jules led them to the center of town square, marching past the statue of a mermaid. The mermaid gazed solemnly out in the direction of the sea. In one hand, she held a shell. In the other, she held what almost resembled a dog's leash.

"She looks sad today," Quincy observed.

"I'm just glad she's here so Dirk can see her," Jules said. "The boardwalk is a long walk away."

"What do you mean?" Davy asked. "Are you saying this statue . . . moves?"

"Well, yeah," Jules said. "It would be pretty boring to stay in the town square all the time, wouldn't it?"

Davy had to admit that was a good point. "I guess so."

The kids continued walking through the square until they reached Main Street. It was lined with perfectly normal things like restaurants, a movie theater, a bank, and a comic book store. A real smile lit up Davy's face.

Maybe Topsea wasn't so strange after all. Maybe it was a regular town with a few extra quirks, and he could get used to living here.

But when they passed the striped pole outside the barbershop, it started spinning—and screaming. Davy covered his ears, alarmed.

"I never realized how much that sounds like Earl Grey!" Jules yelled over the noise.

"No way!" Nia exclaimed. "Earl Grey is *much* louder than that pole!"

The watch hog snorted in agreement.

"But why does the pole scream at all?" Davy hollered right as the pole fell silent. Next to him, Quincy opened his notebook.

"How else would you know when someone's hair is getting cut?" Jules said.

Davy didn't have an answer for that.

"There's the library!" Nia announced excitedly.

Across the street, a large building made of white stone sparkled in the sun. Davy squinted at the two entrances on either side of the building. Each had a sign over the door: BOOK CHECK-OUT and PEOPLE CHECKOUT. "You can check out people?" he asked incredulously. "Why?"

"Why not?" Nia replied as Quincy scribbled in his notebook again. "People and books can both tell stories."

"I guess that's true." Davy couldn't help imagining his dad's reaction to this library. He used to love making up bedtime stories for Davy about robots and aliens and intergalactic battles. He'd probably volunteer to be one of the library's checkout storytellers!

Davy sighed.

Next door, the roof of the post office was covered in seagulls, some of which still had envelopes clamped in their beaks. Davy was kind of used to the seagulls delivering mail by now. But when he saw the big blue mailbox outside the entrance, he halted. Quincy stopped next to him, pen poised over his notebook again.

"Fiction and Nonfiction," Davy read aloud, pointing from one slot to the next. "What does that mean? Is this for the library?"

Instead of responding, Quincy started to scribble.

"What is it that you're always writing, anyway?" Davy asked.

"He's writing down your questions," Jules explained. "You ask very good ones. And these mailboxes are for your mail."

"Fiction and nonfiction *mail*?"

"Well, sure," Jules said. "If you're mailing a letter to your grandmother, it goes in the nonfiction slot. If you're mailing a letter to Rumpelstiltskin, it goes in the fiction slot. I'm pen pals with Gretel."

"*I'm* pen pals with Pinocchio," Nia added.

Jules rolled her eyes. "You are so lying."

Quincy sighed. "I'm still never sure which slot I should put my letter to Santa in."

Down the street, the barbershop pole spun and screamed again. Davy winced. Earl Grey nosed his hand in a comforting way. But despite the kind gesture, Davy didn't feel better. He'd had enough of trying to adjust for one day.

Nia tilted her head. "What's wrong, Devon?"

"Nothing," Davy said. "I—I have to go. I promised my mom I'd help unpack more boxes."

"Aw," said Jules. "We haven't even shown you the bottomless cove yet!"

How can a cove not have a bottom? Davy wanted to ask. Instead, he just said, "Maybe next time. Thanks for the tour!"

His classmates waved good-bye as he headed back down Main Street, and Davy waved back.

He knew he needed to do a better job adjusting. Because he *wanted* to like it here! The library did seem pretty fun. The

endless pier was probably just fine for fishing. The moving mermaid statue was kind of cool, and the screaming barbershop pole . . . well, he could just bring earplugs when he got a haircut.

Sure, none of it was *normal*. But Davy could get used to living in Topsea. If only he didn't miss his old life so much.

From

EVERYTHING YOU NEED TO KNOW ABOUT TOPSEA

by Fox & Coats

The Ice-Cream Man

Everybody loves it when the ice-cream man comes to Topsea.

Even though you never know what you're going to get.

That's the fun of it, most kids say. It's *exciting* when you don't know what you're about to bite into. Whether the flavor on the menu is what you're actually tasting. Or exactly what that crunch is.

Sometimes your ice cream is perfectly normal. At least, it tastes and looks that way.

Sometimes your ice cream is imperfectly normal. Or not normal at all, though you can't always tell at first.

Sometimes, you'll get all the way to the bottom of your ice cream before the surprise.

A candy corn.

A cluster of barnacles.

A plastic triceratops covered in glitter.

A wad of used chewing gum. (Hopefully it's yours?)

The ice-cream truck plays a jingle as it drives around town. All the kids in Topsea recognize it as soon as they hear it, although their parents rarely do. But for some reason, nobody can remember the tune after the truck drives away.

"I think it goes like this," one kid will say, then hum.

"No, that's 'Rockabye Baby.'"

"Are you sure?"

It's the same thing with the ice-cream man himself. As soon as he leaves, nobody can really remember what he looks like, although everybody remembers how *nice* he was.

"He's so smiley! He must be the happiest guy."

"Once my candy-cane-flavored ice-cream cone had a lump of coal in the bottom. But I'm sure it wasn't on purpose."

"I didn't even mind the time I ordered an ice pop, and he gave me a baby-doll head on a stick."

The grown-ups in town have nice things to say about him, too.

"Nothing is as cheerful as the ice-cream truck going by with a crowd of children running after it," they say. They share fond memories of the ice-cream truck from their own childhoods, and all the exciting things they found in their ice-cream cones, like tentacles and elongated molars.

Then again, not everybody likes surprises.

NOTIFICATION: WANTED FLYER

(Posted to every telephone pole in Topsea and stuffed in every mailbox.)

4.

Quincy's Questions

Some kids collect seashells or rocks or oddly shaped teeth. Quincy collected questions.

He kept them in a notebook. Some were questions he asked. Some were questions others asked him. And some were questions he overheard.

Whenever Quincy heard a question, any question, he wrote it down.

So Quincy spent a lot of time writing. He had quite a collection of notebooks, too.

When it came to questions, there was an infinite supply.

It was kind of overwhelming, actually. But then, lots of things overwhelmed Quincy.

His parents asked endless questions at home. And because they were scientists, their questions were especially challenging. Also, Quincy's classmates came to school with shiny new questions every day. This meant Quincy's collection would always be incomplete.

The world would never run out of questions.

Wednesday morning was Show-and-Tell. Quincy brought his questions.

Nia went first. She stood at the front of the classroom holding a hoop. Earl Grey eyed it warily. After the rock-cat incident, Ms. Grimalkin allowed the watch hog in the classroom for special occasions (as long as the kids promised not to tell the PTA).

"Jump!" Nia ordered.

Earl Grey just stared at her.

"Please?" she begged.

Finally, the watch hog leaped toward the hoop. He made it halfway through and got stuck, his back legs wiggling in the air.

Ms. Grimalkin poked his rump with a pointy fingernail. "Looks like someone's been eating too much oatmeal!"

"Snort," protested Earl Grey.

Nia and Ms. Grimalkin pulled and tugged at the hoop until it finally slipped off. With a dignified grunt, Earl Grey trotted out the door, teacup swinging from his curly tail. He reappeared at the window a moment later.

Talise went next. She dragged a huge coil of rope to the front of the class.

"I see you've brought more bathy-matry equipment, Talise," Ms. Grimalkin said.

"I did," Talise said. "And it's pronounced *ba-THYM-etry*."

Quincy smiled. He still wasn't entirely sure what bathymetry was, but Talise did know a lot about the bottom of the ocean. Everyone leaned forward in their desks in anticipation as she cleared her throat.

"This is called a sounding line," she said. "It measures how deep the water is." She stretched the rope out, showing the class the weight tied to one end. The rope had markings like a measuring tape. Talise explained how to throw the weight into the water so it sank to the bottom.

When she finished, Quincy leaned over. "Maybe Talise can find out how deep your locker is, Demetrius," he whispered. "She's great at diving."

"It's Davy," Demetrius whispered back. "Do you think Talise could get my books for me?"

Quincy shook his head. "Locker combinations are top secret. Sharing them is against school rules."

"Quincy, it's your turn to show and tell," Ms. Grimalkin said.

Quickly, Quincy picked up his notebook and headed to the front of the class. He loved watching Show-and-Tell, but presenting made him nervous. His classmates all had such fascinating hobbies, like watch-hog training and bathymetry and investigative reporting. Quincy always struggled to find something as interesting to share.

Pushing his glasses up his nose, Quincy began to read.

"Did you clean your room?

"Is it time for lunch yet?

"When's your birthday?

"Aren't you allergic to that?

"Where does it end?

"Where did that tall man come from?

"Can you please stop writing and just listen?

"Fries or clams?

"Isn't it opening soon?

"Can the PTA do anything to stop it?

"Why is the wall so sticky?

"Did it just lick me?

"Do you hear that scraping noise?

"What's that leaking out from under the door?

"Is that true?

"Is that red?

"Is that what I think it is?

"Did someone just knock?

"Should I answer?"

When Quincy finished reading, the class applauded.

"That's quite a collection of questions, Quincy!" said Ms. Grimalkin. "I'm very impressed."

"Thank you." Quincy felt relieved.

Recess was Quincy's favorite time of the day. During class, Ms. Grimalkin was more interested in answers than questions. And sometimes it was hard to understand questions at lunch, what with all the mouths full of fries or clams. But recess was another story.

The kids ran to the jungle gym to play Walk the Plank. Seaweed Season had just ended, and stubborn strands still clung to the swings, making it hard to swing high. More seaweed hid under the slide, where Quincy knew it was waiting to grab ankles and wrists.

It made him a little anxious. So he sat on a bench and listened, pen poised over his notebook.

"Avast, best matey!" Runa waved a wooden sword and poked Finn, who giggled. "Are ye ready to jump, or should I release the hog?"

Quincy wrote down her question.

Earl Grey trotted forward (a little unsteadily, thanks to his eye patch) and nudged Finn, who hopped off the plank and into the sand. "Ooh!" he said, pointing at his foot. Something glittered in the sand beside it.

"Is that my lost treasure, best matey?" Runa called. "Did anyone warn you that it's cursed?"

Quincy laughed as he added those questions. Runa was always exaggerating and telling tales.

"Do you usually find cursed treasure in the schoolyard?" Davy asked.

Smiling, Quincy added Davy's question, too. Quincy really liked the new kid. He asked lots and lots of questions.

Talise picked up the gold coin by Finn's foot and brushed it off. "Didn't Jules find similar currency last week?"

"Wasn't that a doubloon?" Nia asked.

Jules took the coin from Talise. "No, it was a silver dollar, remember?"

Quincy wrote down Jules's question. He wrote down everyone else's questions, too. Soon his hand started to cramp and his chest felt all tied up in knots. Keeping up with so many questions was stressful!

"What if it really is buried treasure?"

"Can I keep it?"

"Shouldn't Finn get to keep it?"

"Finders keepers, right?"

Suddenly Quincy remembered something. He flipped back a few pages in his notebook and stood up, clearing his throat.

"Has anyone seen my bottle cap?"

"That's right!" Finn piped up. "I lost the cap on my bottle last w—"

"Hang on!" Jules interrupted. "This is a smashed-up seaweed soda cap. Hey, Finn, didn't you lose the cap on your bottle last week?"

Sometimes the other kids had trouble hearing Finn. He sighed and nodded. "Yes. But you can keep it."

"Thanks!" Jules pocketed the cap. "I'll use it at the arcade."

"I thought the arcade was closed," Davy said.

"We know a way in as long as you don't mind spiderwebs," Jules said. "And hey, good investigating, Quincy!"

Quincy blushed.

There was one problem with question collecting: Quincy wasn't nearly as diligent about writing down the answers.

After recess, Ms. Grimalkin pulled down a giant map of the world over the blackboard. "Let's review our lesson on geography," she said. "I hope everyone's been taking notes! Quincy, can you tell us where Vienna is?"

Quincy froze. "Um. Oh. Er."

"Check your notes," Ms. Grimalkin suggested. Quincy flipped quickly through the pages, his heart hammering.

"Have you ever tried Vienna sausages?" he read aloud.

Ms. Grimalkin smiled. "Yes, they're delicious. But the answer is Austria. Let's try another city. How about Brussels?"

Shuffling back a few pages, Quincy scanned more questions. *"Don't you think brussels sprouts smell like dirty socks?"*

"I do," Ms. Grimalkin agreed. "But we're talking about geography, not food. What's the capital of Peru?"

Quincy turned another page. His hands were starting to sweat. *"Are those lima beans?"*

"That is incorrect," Ms. Grimalkin said. "The answer is Lima. Where is Budapest?"

"Hungary," Jules announced, waving her notes in the air.

"Too bad, we already had lunch," Ms. Grimalkin told her. "Quincy, I bet you can answer this one. What is the capital of India?"

"Have you tried the new deli?" Quincy read from his notebook. His voice was shaking now.

Ms. Grimalkin nodded. "Yes, the curry was delicious. But the correct answer is New Delhi. Can you name a city in France?"

"Dijon?" squeaked Finn, but no one heard him.

"Lyon?" Davy tried.

Ms. Grimalkin shook her head. "We already covered animals, Dupin. Quincy, I know you can answer this one! Santiago is the capital of which country?"

"Is the chili vegetarian?"

"No, it's Chile," Ms. Grimalkin said with a sigh. Shaking her head, she rolled the map back up. "I don't understand, Quincy. You take such excellent notes on my questions. Why don't you ever write down the answers?"

Quincy didn't answer. He was too busy writing down her question.

THE TOPSEA SCHOOL GAZETTE

Today's Seaweed Level: Medium-high and feisty

RIDDLE OF THE DAY

What kind of tree do fortune-tellers look at?

(See answer in a future issue)

IT'S RAINING CATS AND CRABS!

by Jules, Fifth-Grade Star Reporter

Today we received an update on the thousands of mysterious crabs that appeared on the beach a few days ago. The crabs have migrated from the beach over to the rocks. So far, the rock cats seem to be getting along really well with the crabs. Which is good news, but also kind of surprising. After all, everyone knows crabs are rock cats' second-favorite meal.

So what's the deal with these new crabs? Why are they here? Where did they come from? What do they want?

As many of you know, this reporter's stepsister is almost a professional journalist. Her advice was to "follow the story"— and that's exactly what this reporter tried to do, until her father caught her sneaking out to the rocks with her sleeping bag last night. Apparently sleeping with the crabs is too "risky," even in the name of journalism. Rest assured, this reporter will come up with another way to study the crabs up close. This story isn't over yet, folks!

A MESSAGE FROM THE PTA

Dairy is very harmful. Many students here at Topsea School are lactose-intolerant. Additionally, it is very easy to choke on a piece of cheddar. Principal King doesn't seem to understand how dangerous this is. Dairy is for cats, not humans! That's why your PTA President is currently circulating a petition to have all dairy banned from school property. Please sign and remember, STAY SAFE!

THE POETRY CORNER

There once was a teacup pig
Who grew to be super big
He's so NOT a dog
He's a clever watch hog!
Even if he ate Nanny's wig.
—Nia

CAFETERIA MENU

~ MONDAY ~

Snack

Milk Sampler

Wry Toast & Chokecherry Jam

Lunch

Mystery Meat (with Clue Sauce)

Stewed Spinach Stew

Milk or Orange Juice

~ TUESDAY ~

Snack

Tomato Juice

Chilled Monkey Bread

Lunch

Seaweed Spaghetti & Mystery Meatballs

Orange or Milk Juice

~ WEDNESDAY ~

Snack

Apple Juice

Applesauce

Apple

Lunch

Crab Cakes

"Cheez" & "Macaroni"

Juice or Orange Milk

~ THURSDAY ~

Snack

Pineapple Juice

Crab Cupcakes

Lunch

Seaweed Burger on a Seaweed Bun with Seaweed Ketchup

Milk or Orangutan Juice

~ FRIDAY ~

Snack

Cranberry Juice

Health Cookie (unless you have cat-hair allergies)

Lunch

Surprising Tuna

Fried Clams, Clammed Fries, or Crammed Flies

Buttermilk (extra chunky)

Finn

Runa

5.

The Chewing Gum Wall

All the kids in Topsea enjoyed Runa's tales. But only Finn believed them.

Well . . . Finn *usually* believed them. He knew his best friend tended to embellish her stories, making them bigger and flashier, adding bells and whistles and glitter and whirligigs. She did the same thing with her artwork. And Finn's hair. (The hot-pink stripes she'd painted in his auburn locks were *finally* beginning to fade.)

But all Runa's stories had some kind of truth at the bottom. The other stuff was just extra fun.

"Did I tell you about the time I painted a dragon?" Runa

asked as they walked to school. "And the room started filling with smoke?"

"Wow!" Finn exclaimed. Not very loudly, of course. Finn lived with a chaos of older brothers, each one louder than the last, and he was used to his small voice being drowned out. But Runa always heard him.

"How about the time I saw a shark fin, way out at sea?" she asked. "Except it was furry and it wagged?"

"Cool!" Finn exclaimed.

As they passed the rocks, she talked about the time she made a huge sand castle on the beach, and when she returned the next day, the rock cats were living inside it. As they neared the school, she described the time her grandparents saw a meteor shower in South Korea, but the stars were all the colors of the rainbow.

"It sounds beautiful," Finn said. He loved rainbows.

"And this other time—" Runa stopped. "Did you hear that?"

"Hear what?"

"A popping sound. I think it came from the chewing gum wall." Runa pointed down a nearby alley.

Finn listened. After a moment, he heard it: *POP! POP!*

"It's like it's calling to us." Runa smiled. "Have you ever seen it up close, Finn? It's gorgeous!"

"Really?"

"Yeah!" Runa grabbed Finn's arm. "Come on, I'll show you."

Finn's older brothers had told him all about the chewing gum wall. Though nobody knew when it had started, everybody figured it'd begun with one wad of gum. One person. Probably not a very nice person. Once a wall is covered in gum, adding another wad doesn't make much of a difference. But when a wall is just a normal wall, sticking your used chewing gum to it isn't very considerate.

Occasionally, one of the parents in town—usually, the President of the PTA—would insist that it needed to be cleaned up.

A biohazard! they'd call it. *Utterly disgusting!*

But cleaning up the chewing gum wall had turned out to be a lot more difficult than it seemed. When Cosmo the janitor had tried, he'd run away screaming. Ricky and Nicky had refused to enter the alley ever again, even after Principal King had offered them a bonus.

"I guess it doesn't really matter," she'd decided. "The chewing gum wall is part of the character of the town. A historical landmark." She'd even considered honoring it with a plaque. But because nobody in Topsea knew when it had started, she hadn't known which date to engrave.

"It's even more gorgeous than I remembered!" Runa said. "Just look at all those swirls and splotches."

Usually, Finn loved how Runa found beauty and excitement in unexpected places. But a wall covered in used chewing gum was taking it a little far. "Yeah, neat," he managed.

Runa sighed dreamily. "It's like a Vincent van Gogh painting."

Finn rubbed his ear. "Maybe."

"Try relaxing your eyes a little bit."

He tried to relax his eyes. The different-colored splotches blurred together. It really did look like a painting, he decided—

like one of Runa's, when she piled on lots of paint. "I guess it *is* kind of pretty."

"I told you!" Runa grinned.

Finn took a step closer. With his eyes still relaxed, the wall appeared to be pulsating. Breathing, even. "It's almost like it's alive."

A bubble rose to the surface with a *POP!*

"Maybe it is." Runa's eyes grew brighter. "Maybe everybody's spit mixed together in some sort of magical science experiment—"

"Magical science experiment?"

"Yes. And it created a new kind of life-form. And it's just waiting for the final piece of gum to bring it entirely to life, so it can slither off the wall and down the street. . . ."

"Dare me to touch it?" Finn asked.

"Eww!" Runa exclaimed.

"It's just gum."

"Gum that's been in other people's mouths." Runa shook her head. "Fine! I dare you to touch it."

Finn's older brothers were always daring him to do things. Usually, he was too afraid. But with Runa beside him, Finn always felt braver. He took a deep breath, narrowed his eyes, and poked the gum with his index finger.

Runa shrieked in laughter. "What did it feel like?"

"Used chewing gum," Finn said.

"Very funny. All right, we'd better get going. The bell's going to ring."

Runa started to walk away. Finn was still staring at the

chewing gum wall. It *had* felt like used chewing gum. But not old gum. This gum was damp and warm, as if it was freshly chewed. Except that wasn't possible, right?

Finn reached out and touched the wall again.

Definitely damp and warm. And sticky. He pressed his whole hand flat against it.

"Weird," he said.

The first bell rang, echoing into the alley. "Finn!" Runa called from the street. "Hurry up! We're going to be late for school. One time I was late, and Principal King had padlocked all the doors, and I had to break into the school's basement and climb through a trapdoor into our classroom. . . ."

Finn pulled his hand away from the wall. The gum stuck to his palm, stretching in gooey, multicolored strings.

"I'll be right there!" he called to Runa.

With his other hand, he tried to scrape away the strings. Gum stuck to that hand, too. He tried to use his foot to push off the wall, but the gum stuck to his shoe. Before long, Finn was entirely covered in chewing gum. He couldn't move.

"Runa!" he shouted.

Runa heard him. She ran back into the alley, skidding to a stop in front of him. "Oh no!" she exclaimed. "Let me help you—"

"Wait! I don't want you to get stuck, too."

Runa pulled back her hand just in time. "I need to find something to pry you loose." She scanned the junk-filled alley. "Ooh! A spork. My favorite utensil."

"Ooh, mine, too," Finn said.

"Maybe that's why we're best friends. Okay, here goes . . ."

Runa jammed the spork into the gum. Instantly, the gum sucked it up.

Finn frowned. He thought he'd heard . . . a *swallowing* sound. "Do you have any other ideas?"

"What about ice water?" Runa suggested. "That's what my mom used when my sister got bubble gum stuck in her hair. You should have seen the bubble! It was bigger than a basketball, and it took five tries to pop it—"

"Runa," Finn said.

"Oh, sorry."

She scampered off. A few minutes later, she came back lugging a bucket.

"The gum stuck in my sister's hair was just one wad," she explained. "But this gum is all over you. Brace yourself."

She tossed the bucket of ice water all over him.

"*Aiiiieee!*" Finn yelped.

"Sorry," Runa said. "Did it help?"

Finn wriggled as hard as he could. Then he shook his head. Or tried to shake his head, since it was stuck to the wall, too. "It just feels like the gum is squeezing me tighter," he said. And now he was also cold and wet, but he decided not to mention it.

The tardy bell rang. "Now we're definitely late," Runa said.

"You go ahead," Finn said bravely. "I'll be okay."

"No way! I'd never leave you."

Finn grinned.

"How about peanut butter?" Runa suggested. "I think that's supposed to help, too."

Runa rooted around in her lunch bag. She always brought

71

her lunch, Finn knew, since she wasn't a fan of the food in the school cafeteria. She pulled out a peanut butter sandwich, opened it, and smeared the peanut butter all over Finn.

"Are those *pickles*?" he asked.

"Just a couple," Runa said. "But did it help?"

"I don't think so. But now I'm hungry." Finn's lower lip quivered. He wasn't feeling brave at all anymore. "What if I'm stuck here past lunch? And dinner? What if I'm stuck here *forever*?"

Runa looked worried. Then her face brightened. "I have another idea! I'll be right back."

"I'll wait for you right here," Finn said.

Runa was gone even longer this time. Finn wiggled his fingers. There was gum between each of them. And between his toes, even though he had shoes on. How was that possible?

He squirmed to the right, then the left. It only made him sink deeper into the wall. The gum really did seem like it was pulsating—even breathing.

In fact, Finn was starting to feel . . . *chewed on*.

"HELP!" he called as loud as he could.

A shadow appeared. It was a person—but not a human.

"Oh, hello there, Earl Grey," Finn said politely. "Do you think you could help me?"

Earl Grey squinted at Finn, as if determining the best way to assist him. Then, snorting happily, he began to lick the peanut butter from Finn's legs.

Finn sighed. Now he was being chewed *and* licked.

At last, Runa returned. "Scissors!" she said triumphantly.

"You really shouldn't run with those," Finn said.

"I'm only jogging." She turned to the watch hog. "Earl Grey! Where did you come from?"

"I think he heard me call for help."

"Wow! Watch hogs must have fantastic hearing. This one time, I was in the beach forest, and it was really quiet, and I— oops, sorry." Runa held up the scissors. "Are you ready?"

"Be careful!" Finn closed his eyes as she jabbed the point of the scissors into the gum, just an inch from his hand.

The gum didn't like that.

Angry bubbles rose to the surface as Runa snipped the scissors. *POP! POP!* She kept snipping. With a damp, squishy hissing sound, the strands of chewing gum pulled away from Finn's hand. He managed to grab Earl Grey's collar.

"Pull!" Finn and Runa shouted.

"*SSCHLORP!*" the gum replied.

With Finn's hand gripping his collar, Earl Grey started forward. It was a game of tug-of-war between the wall and the watch hog. Runa snipped more gooey strings as Earl Grey pulled and pulled.

Finally, with a smacking sound, Finn popped out from the chewing gum wall. He was cold and wet and covered in peanut butter, but the gum was all gone.

"Hooray!" he shouted.

The chewing gum wall looked just like it had before. "You think there'd be a Finn-print or something," Runa said.

"I'm pretty small. Thank you, Runa! You saved me."

"Earl Grey helped, too." She grinned. "What a story. Do you think anyone will believe us?"

Finn grinned back. "It doesn't matter. We believe us."

They gathered up the bucket, and the rest of Runa's lunch. Then they ran all the way to school, with Earl Grey blowing bubbles behind them.

NEW STUDENT SURVEY (SECOND TRY)

by Davy Jones

1. Why did you move to Topsea?

~~My mom made me.~~

My mom got a new job at the seaweed cracker factory. (Why do people eat so much seaweed here??)

2. What are you most excited to learn about at Topsea School, and why?

~~I like math, because it makes sense. But the way Ms. Grimalkin teaches it is weird. She does multiplication tables by scratching them on the wall.~~

I liked our geography lesson, but it made me really hungry.

3. What's your biggest fear?

~~Getting attacked by those rock cats. They give me the creeps.~~

CRABS. And crab—they keep serving it in the cafeteria. The meat is practically black. But for some reason, everyone seems to love it.

4. What's your favorite hobby?

~~Fishing.~~

Skeeball.

5. What's your favorite flavor of ice cream?

~~Pistachio.~~

Nia told me she got bees in her ice cream once! So anything that doesn't have bees is fine with me.

6. Do you have any other thoughts you'd like to share?

I have ALL KINDS of thoughts!

Thoughts about bottle caps. And basements. And crabs! And Monday's milk sampler, which I REALLY wish had been labeled.

But mostly I've got questions. Like: What's in the Untold Caves? (They look scary!)

And: Seriously, what is the deal with those rock cats???

(And: This isn't exactly about Topsea, but what do I do when it's Father's Day? Like if Ms. Grimalkin has us make cards or something, and I'm the only kid without anybody to make a card for?)

And: Will I EVER fit in here?

From

EVERYTHING YOU NEED TO KNOW ABOUT TOPSEA

by Fox & Coats

Basements

Every house in Topsea has a basement.

But not everybody knows how to get to them.

Some basements are filled with old junky things, like model ships in murky bottles. Old beef bones with chew marks on them. Swashbuckler swords and vintage dresses. Rubber ducks with their painted eyes almost rubbed off. Baskets of seashells. Baskets of other kinds of shells. Baskets of oddly shaped teeth. Those basements are the most fun to explore.

Some basements are filled with ocean.

Some basements are filled with nothing. They're just echoey

spaces with moss on the walls, toadstools in the baseboards, and an ever-present smell of seaweed.

Some basements have basements of their own.

Some basements have never been opened. Others were sealed up for a reason, although the owners rarely remember what that reason was.

So how do you find your house's basement?

Well, it's located right below your house.

Most likely, anyway.

But if you want to find a way inside, first make a list of your house's rooms and closets. Even that closet nobody talks about.

Start with the kitchen. Put your ear on the floor and knock. Hear a hollow sound? That's the basement. Keep knocking room by room, closet by closet, until you hear the sound change. That's your basement door!

But wait. Before you get out the jigsaws and skill saws, the handsaws and chain saws, make sure you *really* want to know what kind of basement you have.

And what's inside.

Because that's the thing about basements. They're hard to open. But they're even harder to close.

What you find can't be unfound.

6.

Talise's Tub

Talise was the only kid in Topsea with a deep-sea diving license. Exploring the ocean floor would have been pretty hard without one.

(Except on Vanishing Tide Day, of course.)

If it wasn't for school, Talise probably would have spent more time underwater than on land. She loved the ocean. She needed to know everything there was to know about it—and there was a *lot* to know.

Talise's parents didn't understand her obsession. They also didn't understand why her math and science grades were the best in her class, but she struggled in English and social studies and art.

Talise couldn't explain it either. She studied equally hard for all her classes. Maybe it was because science and math were an important part of bathymetry, and they helped Talise better understand the ocean.

Grades or no grades, Talise's parents were very supportive of her hobby. But one day, they surprised her with something dreadful: an enormous tub where the shower had been.

"It's an extra-deep soaking tub!" her mom said proudly. "We've had the water running all day, and it's finally full."

Talise stared in horror at the steaming tub. It was practically as deep as the school's swimming pool. The drain was a shimmering gray dot.

"Well?" her dad asked. "Do you like it?"

"Of course she does!" her mom told him. "She looks thrilled. Doesn't she?"

They both stared at her expectantly.

Talise's emotions didn't usually show on the outside. Sometimes, that was a good thing. Like when it helped prevent her from hurting her parents' feelings.

Because the truth was, Talise didn't like the looks of this bathtub at all. It was filled with boring regular water, not salt water. And who knew what could be lurking at the bottom? Talise was an ocean expert, not a bathtub expert!

"Thank you," she said politely. "I am very thrilled. Um . . . did you save the receipt?"

"Oh, we didn't buy it," her dad said. "I found it when I was cleaning out the basement. Enjoy your bath!"

Beaming, her parents left her alone with the tub.

Talise sighed. If she was going to take a bath, she needed to prepare.

First, she pulled on her wet suit, flippers, and mask. Next, she strapped on her air tank, regulator, and buoyancy vest. Lastly, she grabbed her depth gauge, underwater compass, and bar of soap. By the time she finished preparing, she was sweaty and in need of a shower.

But all she had was a bath.

Climbing to the edge of the tub, Talise gazed at the water. She considered cannonballing. But that would just get her bath mat all wet. So she stepped off the edge and plunged flippers first into the tub.

The inside of the tub was covered in colorful tile pictures of mermaids and seaweed and toothy cat smiles. Talise sank deeper and deeper, checking her depth gauge every so often. When she passed a tile octopus, the soap slipped out of her hand.

"Drat," Talise said into her regulator, only it sounded like *blarp*. Bubbles streamed in front of her mask.

She consulted her compass and changed direction, following the soap. Her flippers touched the bottom at last. She looked around carefully, mentally listing everything she saw to add to her dive logbook later. A rusty bicycle. An anchor with a broken chain. A glass tortoiseshell. Tortoiseshell glasses.

She flip-flopped over to the drain. Reaching down, she gave the plug a good yank. For a few seconds, she watched a tiny whirlpool form. But then the bar of soap drifted past her fingers. It zoomed straight into the drain, plugging it up again.

"Blarp," Talise muttered into her regulator, only it sounded like *drat*.

Kneeling, she crammed her hand, then her wrist, then her whole arm down into the drain. Her fingers squeezed something squishy.

SQUEAK!

Even underwater, Talise heard it. She let go of the rubber duck instantly. Two more rubber ducks followed the first out of the drain, bobbing and dancing around Talise. They stared at her with rubbed-off eyes.

Talise was not surprised. Rubber ducks with rubbed-off eyes seemed to pop up wherever she went. She found them hiding under the jungle gym at school. Floating in her bowl of cereal. Creeping up the toilet pipes. Once, she'd finished an ice cream only to find rubbed-off eyes gazing at her from inside the cone.

She gathered all the rubber ducks and began to swim back up. When she reached the surface, she heard a knock on the bathroom door.

"Are you *still* taking a bath, Talise?" her mom exclaimed.

Talise took the regulator out of her mouth. "Just finished," she called back. She tossed the rubber ducks into the bucket she kept by the sink.

"I'm glad you like the new tub. But try not to hog the bathroom, honey."

"Okay."

Talise recorded her bath in her dive logbook, then went to bed.

When she woke up the next morning, the tub still hadn't finished draining. But when she checked the bucket of rubber ducks, all she found inside was her bar of soap.

NOTIFICATION: RUBBER DUCK INSTRUCTIONS

Courtesy of the Town Committee for Tideland and

Bath Toy Safety

Digging for clams on the beach is fun! But clams aren't the only things hiding in the sand.

Commonly found objects like glass bottles, rusty coins, and elongated molars are easy to clean and recycle. Other items are much more hazardous to handle—particularly those disguised as innocent toys.

In particular, yellow rubber ducks with the eyes rubbed off.

If you find a yellow rubber duck with the eyes rubbed off buried in the sand, please follow these steps:

1. Fill a bucket with seawater.
2. Wearing protective gardening gloves, place the rubber ducks in the bucket.
3. Store the uncovered bucket in a freezer.
4. During the next Vanishing Tide, take the bucket out on the ocean floor to a depth of at least twenty meters.

5. Turn the bucket over on the sand until the ice block containing the rubber ducks slides out.

6. Leave the ice blocks for the next tide. Return to the coast with the bucket.

Tips:

- For your own safety, do not squeak the rubber ducks.

- Avoid leaving the ice blocks in or near areas with large amounts of seaweed.

- If you're unsure where the ocean floor reaches a depth of twenty meters, consult a bathymetrist.

WARNING! If you find rubber ducks with eyes that aren't rubbed off, contact the Town Committee for Tideland Safety and Preservation immediately. **Do not make eye contact with the rubber ducks.**

THE TOPSEA
SCHOOL GAZETTE

Today's Tide: Fluctuating

WORD OF THE DAY

Troglodyte (n.): Someone or something that lives in a cave (or behaves that way).

MYSTERY CRABS: TO CATCH OR NOT TO CATCH?

by Jules, Fifth-Grade Star Reporter

The Gazette has just received this exclusive close-up photo of one of the new crabs courtesy of Talise, our class bathymetrist and sea-life expert. As you can see, the crab is black with a red smudge on its shell, kind of like a thumbprint. It has sharp pincers near its mouth. Talise recommends you avoid the crabs for now. But if you come across a dead crab, Talise says you should build a basic funeral pyre in your backyard, cremate the crab, and bury its ashes in a sealed clay vial in your basement. Thanks for the tips, Talise!

Meanwhile, this reporter has intensified her search for answers about these mysterious crabs. They're averse to water, which means they probably didn't come from the ocean . . . so where *did* they come from?

As many of you may know, construction workers recently excavated a giant hole in the southwest part of the bluffs in order to expand the still-closed Hanger Cliffs Water Park. This reporter trekked out to the bluffs yesterday to take a peek and now believes they were the crabs' former home. The inside of the hole was strangely sticky, and covered in teeny marks that looked suspiciously crab-claw-like. What's more, those claw marks can be seen leading from the hole all the way out to the rocks.

This reporter's stepsister agrees with her analysis, and added that she is doing an excellent job of investigating and should be very proud of herself. More soon, as the situation develops.

PRINCIPAL'S PRINCIPLES

Hello, students! This is a friendly reminder that the administration, staff, and cafeteria workers have a complete list of student allergies, including lactose intolerance, and would never serve any student a potentially harmful meal. Also, it's possible to choke on any kind of food. But of course, that doesn't mean we can't serve food at all! ☺ Just be sure to chew thoroughly and avoid talking with your mouth full.

We are aware that someone removed all of the coffee creamer from the teachers' lounge and we are working on replacing it as soon as possible.

On a separate note, the PTA no longer has access to the teachers' lounge.

Your Pal,
Principal Josefina (Jo) King

Davy

7.

The Old Arcade

When Davy's classmates asked if he wanted to sneak into the abandoned arcade, he agreed immediately. The "abandoned" part did sound kind of creepy. But Davy was willing to face *anything* for skeeball.

He didn't ask questions when Jules told him rust was afraid of vinegar, then made him rub the smelly stuff all over his arms and legs so the gate wouldn't try to scratch him.

Or when Nia pointed out the patches of seaweed surrounding the arcade most likely to grab his ankles.

Or when Quincy demonstrated the best way to wiggle through the vent without getting attacked by cobwebs.

Of course, Davy *did* have plenty of questions. Could rust really feel fear? Why was the seaweed so grabby? Could cobwebs really attack, or was that just a figure of speech? But he kept these thoughts to himself, because he was adjusting.

Earl Grey was the last to squeeze out of the vent. "We're all in!" Nia said.

Davy looked around. Dried-up seaweed and sand clung to the checkered tile floor. Mold and watermarks covered the walls. "It looks like it got hit by a hurricane," he said. "Is that why this place was closed?"

Quincy sighed. "No, the PTA President closed it years ago."

"Because *rides and games are unsafe*," Nia added in a mocking voice.

"But don't worry," Jules told Davy. "It might be abandoned, but all the games still work. So what's your favorite game?"

Davy grinned. "Well, when my d—"

He stopped abruptly, his smile vanishing.

"Anything's fine with me," he said instead.

"How about pinball?" Finn asked.

Nia jumped up and down. "I have an idea! Let's play pinball!"

Davy followed the others to the pinball machine. But he was still itching to play skeeball.

The pinball game was called Cave Escape. The playfield was a maze of tunnels filled with targets and kickers, spinners and rollovers, switches and stoppers. Finn stepped up to the machine. Jules pulled a smashed-up seaweed soda bottle cap from her pocket and handed it to him.

"Here," she said. "You can borrow this."

Finn said something, but Davy couldn't hear him over Jules and Nia. They were already bickering about whose turn was next. With a shrug, Finn slid the cap into the coin slot and pulled the plunger as far back as it would go. Davy and the others moved closer as he released it, sending the ball zipping around the playfield. Jules and Nia fell silent.

Ping! Ping! Ping! Ping!

PANCK.

Davy blinked in surprise. The ball had somehow frozen in place, just a hair's width from a kicker. Then, impossibly, it started to move *sideways*.

"Is it magnetized?" he asked, gazing as the ball slid slowly toward a spinner.

"Magnets?" Nia laughed. "No. It's the ghost."

"What ghost?"

"The ghost that haunts the pinball machine, silly," Jules told him. "It's not like this is a one-player game."

Davy leaned forward as the ball hit the spinner and ricocheted right into a hole, where it vanished. The lights flashed briefly in triumph before flickering off.

"I wonder if anyone has ever won this game," Quincy said.

Finn made a face at the machine. "Doubt it."

"Doubt it," Jules said at the same time. "That ghost cheats."

The pinball machine lights responded by glowing a dim, ominous red. The other kids stepped back, and after a second of hesitation, Davy did, too.

"Anyway," Nia said nervously. "Let's visit the fortune-teller."

Quincy's face lit up. "Ooh, me first!"

Davy cast a longing glance at the skeeball game in the corner, but followed the others over to the mechanical fortune-teller.

Immediately he decided he wasn't interested in having his fortune told.

The fortune-teller's painted mannequin face was cracked and faded. She had no eyes to speak of. Her mouth was badly chipped, offering a peek into the black interior of her hollow head.

Quincy slipped a few coins into the slot and the machine hummed to life. The fortune-teller's head tilted in a way that reminded Davy of a lizard. He leaned away as Quincy pressed the button below a sign reading MADAM FLEA, TELL ME in fancy, old-fashioned script.

A moment later, a card fluttered down into the tray. Quincy took it eagerly.

What kind of cake worries about its weight?

"Oh, good one." Quincy scribbled the question in his notebook. "I love pound cake."

Nia went next.

What happens to a pig who loses his voice?

Earl Grey grunted in indignation.

"Oh, come on," Nia told him. "It's just a silly fortune, there's no reason to be disgruntled."

"These sound more like riddles," Davy said, watching as Jules pressed the button. "Not fortunes."

"Riddles can be fortunes," Jules informed him. She took her card from the tray.

What do imaginary spiders do in your mind?

Jules sighed. "Oh, that one makes my head spin."

Finn pushed the button and retrieved his card.

What has a spine but no bones?

"Hmm . . ." Finn tapped his chin. "I'll have to look that one up in a book."

Everyone looked at Davy, waiting for him to take his turn. He really didn't want to take a card from Madam Flea. She might not have any eyes, but it felt like something inside her empty head was staring right at him.

But Davy didn't want the others to think he was a chicken. He stepped up and pressed the button, then picked up his card.

What is your name?

Nia's eyes widened. "That's the weirdest fortune I've ever heard, Darcy!"

"I've heard weirder," Jules said. "I'm gonna go try the claw crane. Wanna come?"

Davy slipped the card into his pocket and glanced over at the claw crane. Among the toys inside, he thought he saw a large, black crab shift slightly.

"No thanks," he said. "I think I'll try skeeball."

Finn let out a frightened squeak. The others stared at Davy, mouths open. "Skeeball?" whispered Quincy.

"Sure," Davy said, confused. "It's fun."

"Wow," Nia said, her voice hushed. "You're really brave." Earl Grey snuffled softly in agreement.

Davy stood up a little straighter. "Well, I'm pretty good at it."

He was the Jones family champion, actually. The arcade in his old town had been a little smaller than this one (but mold-free). His mom was great at the claw crane, and his dad had loved Whack-a-Mole. The three of them used to have a standing competition to see who could rack up the most tickets.

"Can we watch?" asked Jules.

Davy smiled. "Sure!"

He led the way this time, fishing around in his pockets for change. To his relief, the skeeball lane looked completely normal. There were holes worth ten, twenty, thirty, forty, and fifty points. When he put his coins in—ten coins for ten rounds—ten balls came shooting down the ramp.

Davy stretched his arms, shook his hands, and wiggled his fingers. Then he picked up the first ball. Keeping his eye on the fifty-point hole, he wound up like a baseball pitcher. His classmates all gasped in unison.

He held the pose a moment for dramatic effect.

Then he tossed the ball underhand. It rolled right up the ramp and landed neatly in the fifty-point hole.

"Yes!" Davy said.

Then he realized the other kids weren't looking at him. They were staring in horror at the slot, from which five tickets had just emerged.

Davy plucked them out. Each one read:

One Prize Coupon
SKEEBALL
Player Must Redeem All Coupons Immediately
Upon Finishing Game
(Or Else)

Shrugging, Davy shoved the tickets in his pocket. Prizes were fine, but they weren't his reason for playing skeeball. The joy was in the game.

Fully aware of his classmates' eyes on him, Davy picked up the second ball. He wound up carefully and pitched.

Once again, the ball fell into the fifty-point hole.

Another five tickets shot out of the slot. This time, Davy ignored them. He landed fifty points with the third ball, fourth ball, and fifth ball, each one earning him another five tickets. He was, as his dad used to say, "in the zone."

Sixth ball. Five tickets.

Seventh. Eighth. Ninth.

Five more tickets each time.

Davy wiped his sweaty hands on his shirt. He picked up the tenth ball, wound up, and pitched. The ball zipped up the ramp and fell perfectly into the fifty-point hole.

"Perfect game!" Davy said proudly.

He looked around to see if his classmates were impressed. Nia's hands were clamped over her mouth. Quincy and Jules were gaping at the long string of tickets protruding from the slot. Finn was attempting to hide behind Earl Grey. Earl Grey was attempting to hide behind Finn.

"Wow," Jules said at last. "How'd you get so good at skee-ball, Daisy?"

"I used to play with . . . um, all the time." Davy swallowed. "In my old town."

"But now you have to claim your prize," Quincy told him. "We can't leave until you do."

"I don't really care about the prize," Davy said. "You can have it if you want." He pulled out the string of tickets and held it out.

The other kids recoiled.

"Sorry, we can't," whispered Quincy. "It has to be you. They're your tickets."

"Oh. Okay." Davy looked around the arcade until he spotted a booth with a sign reading CLAIM YOUR PRIZE HERE. The rusty gate was closed. "But how?" he asked. "There's no one there."

"It doesn't matter." Jules led him over to the booth. The others trailed behind. "You really have a lot of tickets. Aren't you scared?"

"Scared?" Davy repeated. "No. Why?"

"The more tickets, the bigger the prize," Jules said, her eyes wide. She pointed to a slot in the gate. Above it, the counter over a grimy ticket taker was set to *00*. "Go ahead. Slide your tickets in there so it can count them."

Feeling more nervous now, Davy fed the string of tickets into the slot. The counter began to tick up. *01. 02. 03.* No one spoke as it counted all the way up to *45*, then stopped.

For a moment, nothing happened.

Then, slowly, creakily, the gate started to rise. Davy held his breath.

The gate stopped halfway. The darkness inside was so absolute, he couldn't see a thing. But there was a sound.

Scuttling. Scratching.

"What is that?" Davy took a step back. His heart was suddenly pounding very fast.

Jules put her hand on his shoulder. "Your prize."

The *scuttle-scratch* got louder as the thing inside got closer. Davy swallowed hard.

"I don't want a prize," he said loudly. "I changed my mind."

"You have to take it," Jules told him. "It's the rules. This is the prize for forty-five tickets."

"But . . . I don't . . ."

Davy's hands started to shake. Now he could see some sort of movement in the blackness. An unnatural, stilted sort of shifting. "Wait, forty-five? But I had a perfect game!"

Hastily, Davy located five more tickets in his pocket, the ones he got for the first ball. He hurried forward and fed them into the slot. The shifting and *scuttle-scratch* stopped as the counter ticked up.

46. 47. 48. 49. 50.

For a few seconds, there was silence.

Then something fell from behind the gate with a soft but heavy *plop*.

Davy eyed it suspiciously, but it wasn't shifting or scratching. It wasn't moving at all. Finally, he gathered up all his courage, reached out, and touched it.

It was fuzzy.

"Oh, a stuffed narwhal!" Nia cried as Davy pulled the toy from under the gate. "And it's huge! That's a great prize."

With an eager grunt, Earl Grey trotted forward and nuzzled the narwhal. It was nearly as big as he was.

"Why don't you keep it?" Davy said, his hands shaking with relief.

Earl Grey snorted happily. He gently took the stuffed toy between his teeth and trotted back over to Nia.

"Earl Grey is so well behaved now," Quincy said. "He could be a show hog."

"Thanks!" Nia said, then glanced at Jules. "I might have bought a watch-hog training book after all. Sit, Earl Grey!"

Earl Grey set down his new toy and sat with perfect posture, snout in the air.

"I think he really loves that narwhal!" Nia beamed at Davy. "Thank you, Donovan."

"You're welcome," Davy said.

He hadn't felt this happy since moving to Topsea. This arcade was weird and kind of creepy, but he'd still had fun. He'd gone along with what the other kids wanted to do. And he hadn't mentioned his dad at all.

Maybe he'd finally figured out the secret to adjusting!

"Want to play another round?" Jules asked hesitantly.

Davy shook his head. "No, thanks. That was enough skee-ball for one day." He pulled a few more coins out of his pocket, then grinned at his friends. "Let's give that pinball ghost a run for its money!"

THE CARE AND TRAINING OF WATCH HOGS

(Excerpt from the "Training" section)

SHAKE

1. Wear gloves. Hooves can be sharp.
2. Hold a treat in your closed hand. (A glob of oatmeal works best.)
3. When the watch hog points at your hand, grab its hoof and yell "Shake!"
4. Clean up the oatmeal.

ROLL OVER

1. Make sure you are not on a slope.
2. Say "Roll over!" as you twirl your finger around and around and around and around.
3. Eventually, your watch hog will get so dizzy it rolls over.

SPEAK

1. Say "Speak!" and snort, grunt, and squeal as loud as you can.
2. Do this as often as you can.
3. Sooner or later, your watch hog should join in. They are quite fond of duets.

4. But they're even more fond of choruses! Get your friends to snort, grunt, and squeal, too.

JUMP THROUGH A HOOP

1. First, make sure your hoop is larger than your watch hog. (Very important.)
2. Place a bowl of oatmeal on the ground.
3. Hold the hoop between your watch hog and the bowl, and say "Jump!" The watch hog should jump through the hoop into the oatmeal.
4. Hold the hoop higher each time.
5. Eventually, don't put any oatmeal in the bowl.

(Your watch hog will feel a bit betrayed, but will get over it.)

PLAY DEAD

Not recommended! Watch hogs are very sensitive. There is no way to train a watch hog to play dead without hurting its feelings.

SIT ON ROCK CATS

(This section has been scratched out.)

NOTIFICATION: (UN) WELCOME TO TOPSEA

(Posted on the way to Topsea.)

You are now entering Topsea . . .

ATTENTION: ICE-CREAM MAN

*It has been decided (primarily by one very noisy
and unrelenting person) (fine, it's the PTA President)
that it is probably best if you don't visit Topsea anymore.
Many apologies.*
—Mrs. Josefina (Jo) King, Principal of Topsea School
*(who has fond memories of the ice-cream truck from her own
childhood, despite what the Picky Troglodyte Association says)*

8.

Under the Boardwalk

Finn tucked a yellow flower behind his ear, smiling at the sky. It was a perfect afternoon in Topsea. Anything was possible.

"There's nothing to *do*," Nia complained. Earl Grey trotted a couple of feet behind her, teacup dangling from his curly tail.

"What do you usually do on sunny days?" Davy asked.

Quincy jotted down Davy's question in his notebook. "We could go to the beach and look for shells," he said. "Last time I found a scallop shell. And a peanut shell—"

"That sounds great!" Davy was already turning toward the beach.

"Nah, that's boring," Jules interrupted.

Davy turned around again.

Finn giggled. Usually, he felt hesitant when it came to making suggestions. Especially in front of a group. *Especially* without Runa at his side—even just her bright, sparkly presence made him feel like the tallest kid in Topsea.

But today, Finn had a great reason to speak up.

"I brought my glowball!" he exclaimed, pulling it out of his pocket. One of his older brothers had given it to him. When it bounced, it flashed twelve different neon colors. "We could play handball or something. . . ."

"How about we look for the ice-cream man?" Jules suggested. "I haven't seen him in forever."

Nia scoffed. "You don't *look* for the ice-cream man. You listen for him."

"Or catch?" Finn tried.

"We could go back to the arcade," Quincy suggested.

"Maybe Dwayne could win an even bigger prize this time!"

"Glowball," Finn said. "Glowball. Glowball."

Davy gulped. "Um, sure, if you guys want to. Maybe we could avoid the fortune-teller, though? I didn't like the way she was staring at me."

"How could she be staring at you?" Jules said. "She doesn't have any eyes!"

Finn tried a joke: "Like the rubber ducks!"

Nobody heard him. Did they even know he was standing there? Sometimes his friends were just as bad as his chaos of older brothers. Finn sighed and stuffed his glowball back in his pocket.

"Well, standing around here is boring." Nia dropped to one knee. "Race you to the end of the boardwalk! On your mark, get set . . . GO!"

Everybody ran.

Finn ran, too, even though he hated racing. He always lost. Racing isn't any fun when you always lose, since there's no element of surprise. Then again, Nia *loved* to race, even though she always won. Maybe Finn lost at racing because he thought about racing too much while racing?

The other kids were halfway down the boardwalk when Davy stumbled on an uneven plank. Quincy crashed into him. Earl Grey snorted with laughter. So did Jules. "Hurry up, Donnie!" she shouted. "Or the troll will get you!"

"Troll?" Davy asked. "Did you say *troll?"*

"A troll lives under the boardwalk," Finn said.

"A troll lives under the boardwalk!" Jules said.

Everybody in Topsea knew a troll lived under the boardwalk. Well, supposedly. Nobody had actually met the troll in person, but all the kids were a little bit afraid of him.

Davy managed to look anxious and skeptical at the same time. "That's silly. Trolls don't exist."

Nia jumped up and down. "Are you *sure* about that?" Beside her, Jules jumped up and down even higher.

THUMP THUMP THUMPITY THUMPITY—

"HEY!" a voice yelled.

Finn glanced around. "Did you guys hear that?"

Nobody heard him. "Aren't we going to finish our race?" Nia said. "Come on! On your mark, get set . . ."

"Oink!" Earl Grey said.

Giggling, the kids started jogging down the boardwalk again. Finn was about to follow when his glowball slipped from his pocket. "Wait up!" he called, but the other kids kept running.

Bounce went the ball, flashing neon colors.

Bounce

Bounce . . .

Finn dove for it, but he was too late. The glowball rolled through a crack in the boardwalk and disappeared.

"HEY!" the voice yelled again.

It was coming from under the boardwalk.

Finn stood there, frozen. He knew trolls didn't exist, just like Davy had said. Right? Finally, he took a deep breath, crouched down, and peered through the crack in the boardwalk.

A beady eye stared back at him.

Finn leaped back. "Ahhh!"

"HEY!" the voice yelled. "Are you gonna come get your ball, or what?"

By now, the other kids were shimmering dots at the end of the boardwalk. They hadn't even noticed Finn wasn't with them! More than ever, he wished Runa was here. But she wasn't.

Finn would have to retrieve his glowball all by himself.

He swallowed hard, gathering up all his nerve. Then he climbed over the side, dropped onto the sand, and ducked underneath the boardwalk.

"Wow," Finn said. It was much more spacious than he'd realized. But other than the places where sunlight filtered through the cracks, it was pitch-dark. The air smelled of salt and decaying seaweed. "Hello?" he called, dodging a spider web. A crab scuttled over his foot. "Anyone there?"

He didn't expect anyone to hear him.

But the old woman did.

"Over here," she said, switching on a lantern. Her eyes looked like marbles in a face-shaped blob of dough. Her eyebrows were thick and hairy, and her nose was huge. She wore a belted brown tunic, which looked like some kind of animal hide. Around her waist, three square-shaped bells clinked.

She looked like a troll.

And she was holding Finn's glowball. "Is this stupid thing yours?" she grumbled. "It bonked me on the head, you know."

"I'm so sorry," Finn said. "It slipped through the crack."

"Maybe if you kids would slow down, instead of thundering over my roof all day long, you'd manage to hold on to your possessions."

The old woman leaned down and picked up a splintery-looking wooden box, then opened it so Finn could peer inside. It was filled with all kinds of things. Squirt guns. Bow ties. A plastic triccratops covered in glitter. Pencils with chew marks. A ribbon that looked like one of Nia's, or maybe Earl Grey's.

"Everything that falls through the cracks, I hold on to," the old woman said. "But unlike you, your friends never come to retrieve their things."

"They probably don't even realize they dropped them," Finn said.

"Of course not! They're too busy trip-trapping over the boardwalk. Racing through life, day after day. Waking me up from my naps with their loud voices and big, thumpy feet."

"I'm sure they don't mean to," Finn said.

"Why do you keep sticking up for them?" the old woman asked. "Where are your friends right now?"

Finn paused. "Well, they were racing down the boardwalk . . ."

"Of course they were!"

"I don't think they noticed when I stopped. I called to them, but they didn't hear me." Finn frowned. "They never hear me, actually. Almost nobody does."

"I can hear you just fine," the old woman said.

"You can?"

"It's not that hard to hear somebody. As long as you're *listening*."

Finn slipped his glowball into his pocket. He never had any trouble hearing his friends! Although he didn't always hear his brothers—they were so noisy, sometimes he just stopped listening. On purpose. With his fingers in his ears, more often than not.

Finn frowned again. "I need a better way to get their attention."

"What have you tried?" the old woman asked.

"Well, I couldn't find anywhere to rent a megaphone. But I wore clompy boots. I even dyed my hair pink!"

"It didn't help?"

Finn shook his head. "I think my friends get too wrapped up in their own fun. Like when they're being noisy on the boardwalk! Maybe they just need something to snap them out of it."

The old woman stroked her chin, thinking.

Then she unclipped one of the square bells from her belt. "How about you borrow one of these for a while?" she said, handing the bell to Finn. "I use them to scare away rock cats from my supper."

"Thank you!" Finn put the bell in his pocket. Then he plucked the yellow flower from behind his ear and handed it to the old woman.

She tucked it behind her own ear. "Name's Billy, by the way," she said.

"I'm Finn. It's nice to meet you, Billy."

They shook hands.

"Would you like a cup of goat's milk before you go?" Billy asked. "I was just about to pour myself one when your ball bopped me on the head."

"No, thank you," Finn said, wrinkling his nose.

"It's really quite good."

"Some other time."

"Sure thing," Billy said. "And can you do me a favor? If you can get your friends to listen, tell them to slow down. Sounds like they're all wearing clompy boots."

Finn grinned. "I will."

He waved at Billy and ducked out from under the boardwalk. The sudden sunlight made him squint. To his surprise, Nia, Quincy, Davy, Jules, and Earl Grey were waiting for him up above.

"Finn!" they shouted. "Are you okay?"

Finn climbed back onto the boardwalk and hurried to join them. "I'm okay," he said.

"Are you okay?" Nia asked again. "We were so worried about you!"

"We thought the troll ate you," Quincy said.

"She's not actually a troll," Finn said, a little louder. "She's just an old woman named Billy—"

"Did you see the troll?" Jules asked. "What does he look like?"

Finn sighed. Nothing had changed. Even if his friends had come back for him, they still weren't listening to him.

Then he remembered Billy's bell.

"So what do you guys want to—" Nia began.

Finn shook the bell as hard as he could: *CLANGCLANG-CLANG*. All his friends shut up and stared, even Earl Grey.

"You guys never listen to me," Finn said.

"Oh!" Nia said. "Sorry."

"You just have a quiet voice, is all," Quincy said.

Davy nodded in agreement. "Abnormally quiet."

"I know I do." Finn sighed. "But it happens all the time. If you slowed down and listened, like Billy said, maybe you'd hear some of my ideas. And jokes! Sometimes I make funny jokes!"

"Wait, who's Billy?" Quincy asked.

"Hang on," Jules said. "How about Finn decides what we do for the rest of the afternoon? You know. To make up for his ordeal."

Finn beamed. This was what he'd been waiting for! "I think we should—" he began. "Oh, wait! First, I'm supposed to tell you . . ."

Then he paused.

He couldn't remember what he was going to say.

THE TOPSEA SCHOOL GAZETTE

Today's Tide: High

REMINDER: The synchronized swim team's after-school practice has been moved to the soccer field.

NIGHTY-NIGHT, CRABS

by Jules, Fifth-Grade Star Reporter

Breaking news! The thousands of strange black crabs are leaving the rocks. Sort of. According to Talise, the crabs are digging deep into the sand under the rocks, where they will probably hibernate like bears or cave bats. This does tell us a lot about these crabs' preferred habitat—unlike regular crabs, who live in the ocean, these crabs clearly prefer the dark and dry of underground burrows. This might also explain why they have a softer exoskeleton than most crabs.

Everyone keeps insisting that there's nothing weird about these crabs. But this reporter's stepsister said she should always follow her instincts—and her instincts say there's more to this story. So this reporter isn't giving up until she uncovers the truth. Stay tuned!

A MESSAGE FROM THE PTA

This is a reminder to students that school is a place for answers, not questions. Questions can be very dangerous, especially for young minds. If you need answers, please consult your textbooks or a PTA-approved fortune-teller. Remember: think before you ask, then don't ask. STAY SAFE!

9.

Runa's Tales

Life in Topsea could be a whole lot of fun. Like during Seaweed Season. Or Gravity Maintenance. Or after an Extremely High Tide hit, when Runa and her sister could gather starfish right from their front lawn.

But with a little embellishment, life could be even *more* fun, you know? A few extra colors and details, some trumpet fanfares, an extra troll or two.

That's what Runa thought.

But Ms. Grimalkin felt differently. "Runa, you know I love your tales," she said as she handed back her English paper.

"Thanks!" Runa said. She'd written about her summer

vacation, which she really had spent in South Korea . . . although there hadn't actually been any flying tigers.

"But there's a right time and place for telling them," Ms. Grimalkin continued.

"What do you mean?" Runa asked.

"When you're always telling tales, it's hard to separate the truth from fiction. Have you ever heard of the boy who cried wolf?"

Runa brightened. "No, but I've heard of a boy who was raised by wolves! He lives in the beach forest, and has sticks and leaves in his hair, and one day I was looking for pinecones for an art project and he *howled* at me—"

Ms. Grimalkin sighed. "Never mind."

After English came art, which was Runa's all-time favorite subject. Ms. Grimalkin let the kids work on whatever they wanted. Finn was making flowers from crepe paper. Quincy was working on a collage of question marks clipped from old magazines. Nia was making a tutu for Earl Grey.

"Hold still," Nia ordered, knotting another piece of tulle around the watch hog's substantial waist.

Talise was making a scientifically accurate undersea diorama. Jules was sketching cartoons for the school paper. Davy was sculpting a dog from clay, which made Runa smile.

She pulled out her latest painting. This one was abstract, the canvas piled with thick, colorful paint. She'd wanted it to look like a van Gogh painting. But it looked more like the chewing gum wall, if you relaxed your eyes.

"What's that supposed to be?" Jules asked.

"The night sky," Runa said. "More specifically, this one time I saw a meteor shower, but all the stars were rainbow colors, and the entire sky looked like a swirly rainbow—"

"Suuuuure," Jules said with a grin.

Runa heard that word a whole lot—especially from Jules, who preferred facts to fiction. So Runa was used to it. But that didn't mean she *liked* it.

"I think it's pretty!" Nia said.

Runa beamed at Nia, then turned back to her painting. "Oops," she said. "I'm out of paint."

"Maybe if you didn't use so much of it," Jules said.

"It's called alla prima," Runa said. "Paint looks better when it has lots of texture."

"But does it really need to be six inches thick?"

"I like it," Finn said. "It's like . . . a mountain range in the sky."

"Thanks!" Runa decided she'd give him the painting when she was finished. Finn always appreciated her artwork, unlike some of the other kids. Once, she'd tried to give Quincy a painting of the ocean. He'd said, "Um. Oh. Er. Thanks, but I don't think I have anywhere to put it." Maybe because the seaweed she'd used had still been a little wriggly?

"Is there any more paint?" Runa asked Ms. Grimalkin.

"Looks like we're all out." Ms. Grimalkin opened her desk drawer and pulled out a skeleton key. "Would you mind visiting the storage closet to get some?"

"Sure," Runa said. "Where is it?"

"In the basement."

Runa gulped. She wasn't afraid of much, but she'd never been in the basement of Topsea School. And since the school was very large, she had the feeling the basement would be very large, too. "Do you have a map?"

"Don't be silly," Ms. Grimalkin said. "I'll just give you directions. Are you ready?"

"I guess so."

"Take your first left, then second left, then third right, then first left. Go all the way to the end of the hall, and take the stairs down—the long staircase, not the short one. Turn right again. On your left, you'll find a set of double doors. After that, another staircase leading down. Turn left, right, second right, then straight on until you find the locked closet door. There will be another locked door behind it. At the bottom of the stairs you find, there'll be a third locked door. That's the art supply closet!"

Runa rubbed her temples. "Did you say 'left' after the long staircase?"

"Right," Ms. Grimalkin said.

"Okay. I think I've got it."

"Why don't you take a buddy with you?"

"Good idea!" Runa smiled at Finn.

But then Ms. Grimalkin tapped Davy on the shoulder. "How about you?" she asked him.

Runa's smile flipped upside down. *"Donny?"*

"Be kind," Ms. Grimalkin said. "His name is Dolly."

Davy blushed. "Sure, I'll go."

Finn looked a little jealous, but he patted Davy on the head. "Runa's the best," he said. "If you're lucky, she'll tell you a story!"

"Lucky?" Jules repeated. "Storytelling is all Runa *does*."

"Clearly, she paints as well," Talise said.

Runa smiled at Talise, then side-eyed Davy as they headed into the hallway. When she was in the middle of a tale, she didn't care who believed her. But she felt a little self-conscious in front of the new kid. Who knew what kinds of glittery, whirly, fantastical things he'd seen in his old town?

As soon as they entered the hallway, Runa got down on her hands and knees and started knocking on the floor. She crawled a few feet and knocked again. "Does that sound hollow to you?" she asked Davy.

His brow was furrowed. "What are you doing?"

"I'm trying to find the basement, obviously."

"Isn't it right over there?" Davy pointed at a green door.

"Oh," Runa said, getting to her feet. "That probably leads to the basement."

TO BASEMENT

She used Ms. Grimalkin's skeleton key to unlock the door. As they started down the steps, Davy looked nervous.

"Did you really remember Ms. Grimalkin's directions?" he asked. "Because I probably only heard a fifth of them."

"Which fifth?" Runa asked hopefully. "I'm pretty sure I've got the first and fourth fifths. If you got one of the other fifths, we'll be a whole lot closer to a whole."

Davy shrugged. "A bunch of left turns. A bunch of right turns. Something about a set of double doors . . ."

"Perfect!"

Runa wasn't sure what she'd expected the school's basement to look like. Maybe dark and drippy and dungeonlike, with flickering candles, and strange symbols painted on the moss-covered walls . . .

That's the tale Runa would have told.

But the basement was brightly lit. Fluorescent lights overhead made a buzzing sound. Occasionally, they heard a beeping, but they couldn't tell where it was coming from. Everything smelled like bleach.

As Runa and Davy wound down stairs and through hallways, they passed numerous doors. They all had boring names:

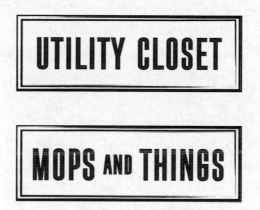

None of the doors said STORAGE CLOSET, though. Runa did her best to follow Ms. Grimalkin's directions. But she knew she and Davy were lost long before she admitted it—first to herself, and then to Davy, who was plodding along beside her like a trusty dog in a storybook.

"I don't know where we are," she confessed.

"Uh-oh." Davy stopped. "Are you saying we're lost?"

"Well . . . I wouldn't say lost, exactly. I think I know how to move backward. But not forward."

"I guess we'll have to return without the paint."

Runa took a few steps backward, then sighed. "I don't want to disappoint Ms. Grimalkin."

"Why don't you tell her the truth?" Davy asked. "I mean, that you forgot her directions?"

"She'll think I'm making it up," Runa said. "If you haven't noticed . . . I tend to exaggerate from time to time."

"But why would you lie about something like *that*?"

Runa squinted. "Well, why would you lie about your name?"

"I'm not lying! My name really is Davy."

"Suuuuure," she said.

Davy rolled his eyes. Runa hoped she hadn't hurt his feelings. Boys could be so *sensitive*.

"You and I make kind of a funny pair, don't we?" he said as they backtracked through the basement.

"A pair?" Runa repeated.

Davy's cheeks turned a little pinker. "I just meant, we're opposites. I'm always wishing everything in Topsea was *less* strange. And you're always inventing stories to make it even stranger!"

Runa giggled. "That's true! But it's so much more fun that way, you know?"

"I do, actually. I mean, I've never told many stories, but— my dad used to tell really great ones. About intergalactic battles and aliens and robots."

"Wow!" Runa said. "I bet I'd like your dad."

Instead of replying, Davy blinked at his shoes. His cheeks went from pink to red. Runa hoped she hadn't said something wrong again. It wouldn't be the first time.

"It'd be nice if people believed me when I wanted them to, though," she went on. "Like the time Finn got stuck to the chewing gum wall, and the only tool I could find to help him was a spork . . ."

Finally, they made it back to the classroom. "Greetings, basement spelunkers," Ms. Grimalkin said. "Did you manage to locate the paint?"

But before Runa could answer, all the other kids in the class crowded around them.

"I can't believe you went in the basement!" Nia exclaimed, bouncing excitedly in place.

"I'd have been so nervous," Quincy said. "What kind of stuff was down there?"

"No bathtubs, I sincerely hope," Talise added.

Runa glanced at Davy. Then she glanced at Ms. Grimalkin, who was listening closely. "Well . . . nothing much, actually. Just a lot of fluorescent lights—"

"In all kinds of colors," Davy interrupted. "Flickering and flashing in every color of the rainbow!"

Runa stared at him. "Huh?" she mouthed.

"Cool!" Jules said.

"And we passed all kinds of swirly, creepy staircases," Davy continued. "Secret passageways and trapdoors and booby traps. Doors with really weird things on them. Like . . . CLOWNS. And ODDLY SHAPED TEETH. And DRAGONS!"

"Dragons?" Nia exclaimed. "Wow! You guys are really brave."

Runa grinned at Davy. "Thanks, Doogie."

Davy grinned back, his cheeks pink. "No problem."

Runa felt a tap on her shoulder. She turned to find Finn, looking a bit left out. "Will you take me next time?" he asked. "The basement sounds so cool!"

"Ehhh," Runa said. "Doogie was just telling tales."

10.

Tide Pools

"There'll be a Severely Low Tide all week," Ms. Grimalkin announced, adjusting her tortoiseshell glasses. "Which means it's the perfect time to study tide pools."

Studying the ocean all week? Talise was thrilled!

Well, as thrilled as Talise ever was. As usual, it was hard to tell from the outside, but she definitely felt thrilled on the inside.

The rest of the class was thrilled on the outside. They skipped and laughed during their walk to the beach, which didn't take long. Seagulls dipped and cawed overhead, and rock cats glowered from their perches. Talise didn't pay them any attention, though. The ocean was all she cared about.

Ms. Grimalkin passed out identification guides. "Now everybody pick a tide pool to monitor for the week," she said. "There should be exactly enough for everyone in the class."

Everybody scampered toward the tide pools.

"I pick this one!" Jules yelled.

"No fair, I wanted that one." Nia pouted, then perked up. "Wait, this one's even better."

"No it's not," Jules said. "Is it?"

"Ooh, this tide pool is shaped like a heart," Runa said. "Finn! Come get the one beside mine—it looks like a lung. In fact, I'm pretty sure it's breathing. . . ."

Talise was excited to pick out her tide pool, too, even if it didn't show on the outside. But she needed to put on all her equipment beforehand.

First, she pulled on her wet suit, flippers, and mask. Next, she strapped on her air tank, regulator, and buoyancy vest. Last of all, she grabbed her depth gauge, underwater compass, and waterproof notebook.

"Talise, what are you doing?" Ms. Grimalkin asked.

"Blurp blop bloop?" Talise replied.

"What?"

Talise spit out her regulator. "I said, I thought we were monitoring tide pools?"

"Yes, but you'll be observing them from the outside, not the inside. You don't need an air tank for that."

"Drat," Talise said.

By the time Talise had put away her wet suit, flippers, mask, air tank, regulator, buoyancy vest, depth gauge, underwater compass, and waterproof notebook, there was only one tide pool left unclaimed. She hurried over to it and peered inside.

"Excuse me, Ms. Grimalkin?" Talise said.

"Yes?"

"There appears to be nothing in my tide pool."

"That can't be true. I checked them all this morning." Ms. Grimalkin came over and pointed. "See? There's a creature right there."

Talise squinted. Sure enough, she spotted a weird, slimy lump wedged under a lip of stone. It was the most unattractive thing she'd ever seen. And Talise had seen her share of unattractive things. A rotting stonefish. A giant spiderweb filled with crabs. Her dad before coffee.

With a sigh, Talise skimmed her identification guide, trying to locate the slimy, lumpy creature. *Sea cucumber* was close. *Sea slug* was closer, but still not quite right.

"Hmm," she said.

Then, at the very bottom of the page, she recognized it.

SEA BLOB

"A sea blob?" Talise said, feeling dismayed. "That's the worst thing."

The list of sea-blob characteristics was even less inspiring:

Diet: mud.
Size: medium.
Color: medium.
Personality: none.

Talise glanced around at her classmates. They were all peering into their tide pools with grins on their faces. Each of them was thrilled on the outside.

"One of my fish just did a backflip!" Jules exclaimed.

"One of mine did a double backflip!" Nia exclaimed even louder.

"Anybody want to trade?" Talise asked.

Nobody replied. Resigned, Talise turned back to her own tide pool. The sea blob was pulsating slowly. *Pulsating*, she wrote in her notebook. *Blobby*.

"Am I allowed to poke it?" she asked Ms. Grimalkin.

"No," Ms. Grimalkin said.

Talise frowned at the sea blob. It frowned back at her. But maybe that was just the way its face looked? She wondered if her face always had the same expression, too. She tried smiling at the blob. It frowned back at her.

The next day, Talise was the first kid to the beach. She ran right to the tide pool beside hers, sat down, and crossed her legs.

"Well, this is a positive turn of events," she declared. "My tide pool is a whole lot more interesting today. Sea stars. Psychedelic eels. All kinds of anemones, wow."

"That's because it's my tide pool," Quincy said.

"Do you have any proof?" Talise asked.

Quincy opened his notebook, where he'd written:

Sea stars
Psychedelic eels
All kinds of anemones, wow

"Drat," Talise said. She trudged over to her own tide pool, where the sea blob waited. She sat down, staring at it.

Nothing happened.

Talise decided to try talking to it. "Greetings, Sea Blob," she said. "My name is Talise. Would it be possible for you to *do* something? Anything? A tiny little backflip, perhaps. Or even just a quick lap around the pool . . . ?"

The sea blob pulsated. Talise assumed that meant no.

"Here's my concern," she went on. "I really need to get an A. Science is the only subject I'm good at, besides math. In fact, I'm superlative at science. Quite possibly the best in the entire class. But if I fail this project . . . then I won't be."

The sea blob didn't reply.

Talise continued. "I'm already doing so poorly in English. And social studies. And art. Which shouldn't even be an official subject, if you ask me—"

"Hey!" Runa exclaimed.

"Whoops, sorry." Talise lowered her voice. "If I could, I'd be down there all the time. Like you get to, huh? It must be nice to be a sea blob."

She looked at the sea blob.

"I take it back," she said.

"Are you talking to your tide pool?" Quincy asked.

On the inside, Talise felt slightly embarrassed. "Only a little."

"Great idea!" Quincy leaned over his tide pool. "Hi there, all you funny little sea thingies. How are you doing?" He giggled. "Hey, they all started blowing bubbles! Do you think they actually hear me? This is so much fun!"

Talise sighed.

The next day, she shuffled to her tide pool with her hands in her pockets. The sea blob still hadn't moved. Its slimy coating had shifted a bit, but that was all.

Talise's insides started to feel angry.

Stupid slimy sea blob! The most boring creature in all the ocean! Science was the only subject Talise loved, and now she was going to get a big, fat F on this project! A project about the *ocean*! Her parents would never understand that it was all the sea blob's fault!

She glanced around. Nobody was looking. They were all watching their own tide pools. Ms. Grimalkin was standing beside Quincy. "Your fish look so delicious," she told him. "Oops—I meant delightful."

Talise took a deep breath.

Then she reached into her tide pool and poked the sea blob as hard as she could.

SQUEAK!

The rest of the slime fell away, revealing a rubber duck.

"Oh, come *on*," Talise said with a groan.

All the other kids crowded around Talise's tide pool to look. "Are its painted eyes rubbed off?" Jules asked, covering her own eyes.

"They are!" Nia exclaimed. "Thank goodness."

"Anybody have a bucket?" Quincy asked.

"I do in my desk," Runa said. "Want me to run back and get it?"

"Thank you, Runa, that would be very helpful." Ms. Grimalkin patted Talise on the shoulder. "I'm sorry your tide pool was such a dud. I had no idea."

"That's okay," Talise said.

"It isn't, really. I'm giving you ten points extra credit for your patience. Why don't you share Daymond's tide pool for the rest of the lesson?"

Talise went and stood beside Davy. His tide pool was bustling with activity. "What have you identified so far?" she asked.

"Only a few things." Davy handed her his notebook.

Talise flipped through it, frowning, then laughing. "That's not a brittle star! It's a monkey squid. See, you know because of its little face. And all those invertebrates on the left are rainbow shrimp, not sea crickets." She showed him in her identification guide.

"Wow, you're right," Davy said. "You really do know a lot about the ocean."

Talise grinned so hard her face ached. For once, she was thrilled on the outside, too. "Indeed. I really do."

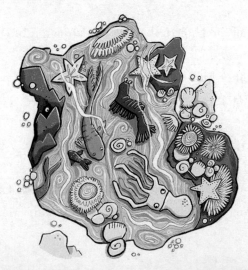

Davy

11.

Abnormally Normal

"You're certainly in a good mood this morning," Davy's mom said, handing him a heaping bowl of cornflakes.

Davy realized he'd been humming. "Oh," he said, blushing a little. "I guess I am."

"Are you feeling more comfortable in Topsea?"

"I guess so." He dug through his cereal with his spoon, checking for wayward seaweed. Just another part of coastal life, he knew. But that didn't mean it wasn't *weird*. "It still doesn't feel normal, though."

"I know what you mean." His mom sat beside him and

started digging through her own bowl. "But imagine if we'd moved here from a big city. Or another country! So many people move every day without knowing the culture, or even the language."

"It'd make it a lot harder to adjust," Davy said thoughtfully. "And to make friends. Luckily, that part's been pretty easy here."

"That's wonderful!" His mom beamed.

"At least, I *think* they're my friends. They still can't remember my name." Davy plucked a piece of seaweed from his bowl and set it on his napkin. Immediately, it wriggled off the table and onto the floor.

His mom stomped on it. "My supervisor at the seaweed cracker factory called me Bartholomew for a week. They probably just need to get to know you better."

"They do know me!" Davy paused. "Sort of. Maybe I'm just not memorable enough. They're all so interesting, and I'm so . . . *normal*."

"Well, *I* think you're special."

He rolled his eyes. "Thanks, Mom."

She ruffled his shaggy brown hair. "You know what your dad would have told you?"

"He'd want me to try new things," Davy said. "And I have been! I've done all sorts of crazy, wild stuff. I raced across the boardwalk with a troll underneath. I got lost in the school's basement. I snuck into the abandoned arcade—"

"Wait, you *snuck in*?"

Davy busied himself with his bowl of cereal.

"I'll pretend I didn't hear that," his mom said. "Sure, your dad thought trying new things was important. But that doesn't always mean crazy, wild things."

"Then what does it mean?"

"It can mean anything at all. Even something as small as a pickle-and-peanut-butter sandwich." She smiled, though there was a bit of sadness in it. "Or even just trying out new hobbies. Your friends find them interesting. If you never try them yourself, how will you ever know why?"

Davy scratched his head.

He'd thought Runa's outrageous tales were weird. But when he'd tried telling them himself, all the other kids had been fascinated! He'd felt interesting *then*, even if it was only for a few minutes.

And anytime he'd joined in the activities his friends suggested, like at the arcade and on the boardwalk, he'd had a great time.

In fact . . . he'd felt almost *normal.*

Acting like a Topsea kid made Davy feel like a Topsea kid. Why hadn't he realized that before?

"Great idea, Mom!" Davy exclaimed. "I'll act exactly like my friends!"

His mom raised an eyebrow. "I don't know if you need to act *exactly* like them. . . ."

But he was already rushing out the door.

Since moving to Topsea, Davy had spent the most time with Quincy. And every day, all day, he'd watched his new friend write down questions. Hundreds of questions! Although Davy had no idea *why* Quincy did it, his hobby seemed like an easy place to start.

First, Davy stopped by the drugstore for a new notebook.

"I'm sorry," said the shopkeeper. "We just sold our last notebook to another kid."

"Aw, nuts," Davy said. "I'll bet he had red glasses. Do you have anything else I could use for writing things down?"

"You're in luck!" The shopkeeper reached under the counter and handed Davy a roll of paper, a pot of ink, and a gigantic peacock feather. "Will this work?"

Davy blinked. "Oh. Um. Er." This wasn't anything like Quincy's notebook! But Davy didn't want to quit before he'd started. "I guess I'll take them."

The first kids he spotted were Runa and Finn, sitting on swings in the schoolyard. "Hey Ru—" he began, then remembered his gigantic feather.

He dove behind a tree.

At least he could still hear their conversation. Well, he couldn't really make out what Finn was saying, as usual. But Runa's questions were loud and clear. In fact, practically everything she said was a question! Davy wrote them down as quickly as his feather pen could go:

Did I tell you about the time I found the end of the endless pier?

And I fell off the end?

And a nice, gentle tidal wave carried me back to shore?

What about the time I saw the mermaid statue get up and walk across town?

"Mermaids don't walk," Davy muttered to himself, then paused. "Wait—neither do statues."

And then she started singing the most beautiful music?

And all the rock cats started yowling along?

"What are you doing?"

What are you—

Somebody bopped Davy on the head. He dropped his pot of ink, then held his peacock feather in front of his face.

"Are you eavesdropping?" Jules demanded.

Davy lowered the feather. Nia stood beside Jules, hands on her hips. Even Earl Grey appeared to be glaring.

"Sit," Nia said to Earl Grey, who sat down immediately. Then she turned to Davy. "You're spying!"

"What?" Davy said. "No I'm not."

Jules peered at him. "Why should we believe you, Doug? You're still new in town. You might have an ulterior motive."

"What does that even mean?"

"It—" Jules began. "I'm not actually sure."

"Have you discovered any big secrets?" Nia asked. "The top-secrety kind? Oh, you've *got* to tell us!"

"I'm not a spy!" Davy said. "And anyway, Jules is always writing down stuff, too."

Nia slung an arm around Jules's shoulders. "That's because Jules is a star reporter!"

"That's right!" Jules grinned. "And Nia is . . . um, a star athlete. And my very best friend."

"Really?" Davy said. "You guys bicker nonstop."

Nia scowled at him. "No we don't!"

"Yes, we do," Jules bickered.

"What were you really writing?" Suddenly Nia's face brightened. "Were you writing *poetry*? Oh, I love poems! Can you read us one?"

Davy turned magenta.

The whole time, Earl Grey had been sitting politely a few feet away. Nia really had done a great job training him. Davy had never trained a pet before—he'd always wanted a dog, but his dad had been allergic. . . .

"I know!" Davy said. He thrust the feather, pot of ink, and scroll at the girls.

"You know what?" Nia asked.

"What do you know?" Jules asked.

But Davy was already sprinting for the beach.

When he neared the rocks, he slowed. Pet cats were perfectly normal in Davy's old town. But by now, he was pretty sure the rock cats weren't normal cats. They stared back at him with their yellow eyes, making him feel uneasy. Could they tell Davy was more of a dog person?

Then he saw a crab scuttling over the rock closest to him. It paused to look at him, tapping its triple-jointed legs as if in greeting.

"Even better!" Davy said, relieved.

Cautiously, he reached out. The crab jumped right onto his arm. Its numerous pointy legs tickled his skin, giving him a shivery feeling. Topsea crabs were creepy looking, but they didn't have great big claws, like normal crabs. They had tiny pincers on either side of their mouths.

"Sit," Davy said, in the same tone Nia had used with Earl Grey.

The crab crawled up his shoulder and into his hair.

"Ahhh!" He shook his head. The crab fell out onto the sand. "Sit!" he ordered even more loudly.

The crab scuttled toward the rocks and disappeared.

Davy sighed. He walked along the beach with his head down, feeling discouraged. Who else could he try to be like?

There was Talise, who knew so much about the ocean. It was amazing! But Davy didn't have any bathymetry equipment, let alone a scuba license. He'd always thought he'd get one with his dad someday.

He could paint, like Runa. But his paintings would never be as good as her beautiful ones. Or her tales. They were almost as good as the ones his dad used to tell.

He could try to talk really quietly, like Finn. But he was pretty sure nobody would notice.

He could tie a teacup to his tail, like Earl Grey. . . .

Davy sighed. He didn't have a tail.

It was no use. Davy had thought acting like his Topsea friends would make him feel normal. And once he felt normal, life would go back to normal again. But now he knew that was impossible.

"What's the trouble, buddy?"

Davy glanced over. It was Ricky, the cafeteria man with the knife-and-fork tattoo on his bicep. He was holding a shovel.

"Oh," Davy said with a gusty sigh. "I was just thinking."

"About something pretty depressing," Ricky said, "judging from a sigh like that."

Davy shrugged. "What are you doing with that shovel?"

"Digging for clams. And other things."

"Other things?" Davy repeated. "Like what?"

Ricky winked. "Who knows? But that's the fun of it. It's just like when the ice-cream man comes to town—you never know what you're going to get."

"I've never tried Topsea ice cream," Davy admitted.

"No? Well . . . that might not be a bad thing."

Davy shrugged. He knew he probably wouldn't like it. Actually, he'd probably be afraid to take a bite, after the rumors he'd heard. And even if he did take a bite, he'd probably compare it to ice cream back home.

Ricky plunged his shovel into the wet sand. It hit something with a *PANCK*. "Uh-oh," he said. "Better not dig here—"

"The trouble is, I'm just too normal!" Davy exclaimed.

"Normal?"

"I'm the only normal kid in all of Topsea," he went on in a rush. "Everyone here is so different, but in these unique, wonderful ways. Everyone except me. The normal one. From a normal, boring town."

"Hmm," Ricky said. "Did you live in a high-rise apartment? Or a Bedouin tent?"

Davy squinted. "Huh? No. It was just a normal house. In a normal town."

"Was it carved into a mountainside, or built on a floating island on top of a lake?"

"Well, it was *beside* a lake—"

"When you looked out the window, did you see baobab trees

or Joshua trees? Were there giraffes and two-toed sloths, or penguins and spider monkeys?"

"There weren't any of those things!" Davy said, feeling frustrated. "It was just a normal town with normal kids in it."

"So you were all exactly the same?"

"Well . . . no. Not exactly."

"I'm just trying to figure out what you mean by *normal*," Ricky said with a wink. "I'm not sure there's any one definition, is there?"

Davy thought about that. "I guess even a village carved into a mountainside is normal to the people who live there. The way my old town was normal to me. And Topsea is normal to you."

SSCHLORP! Ricky pulled his shovel out of the sand. A giant wad of chewing gum was stuck to it. "Yep," he said. "Totally normal."

"You know what's funny?" Davy went on. "When I think about it . . . back then, I didn't *feel* normal. In fact, I felt like everyone was normal except me. I didn't always feel that way, though. Just ever since . . ."

Ricky waited.

"Ever since my dad passed away," Davy finished.

"I don't think that's very funny," Ricky said, leaning on his shovel. "But I understand."

"And now I'm living in a brand-new town—but instead of being the not-normal one, I'm the only normal one! I just can't win!"

Ricky chuckled. "Now *that*, I think, is funny."

Davy frowned. "Why?"

"If being normal makes you not-normal in Topsea—well, maybe you're closer to Topsea normal than you think."

"Hmm," Davy said.

But the more he thought about it, the more true it seemed. If Davy was the only normal kid in a not-normal town . . . didn't that make him just as unique as the other kids? They all stood out in their own weird, wonderful ways. And from their perspective, maybe Davy did, too.

Even if what made him different ached a little bit.

"Have you talked to your new friends about your dad?" Ricky asked, as if reading his mind.

"Not really," Davy replied.

"I bet they'd be happy to listen."

The idea made Davy's stomach feel twisty-turny, just like it had on his first day of school. He was pretty sure his new friends would listen if he brought up his dad. But was Davy ready?

"I'll think about it," he said.

Ricky stretched. "Work sure makes me hungry." He reached into his apron and pulled out a couple of foil-wrapped bundles. "Would you like one of these crab cakes? They're cold—but even better that way, if you ask me."

Davy hesitated. Then he shook his head and smiled. What was he so afraid of, anyway? Like his mom had said, trying new things could mean something as small as a pickle-and-peanut-butter sandwich. Or a crab cake.

"Sure!" Davy said, accepting a foil bundle.

He unwrapped it, hoping none of the crabs were watching. He took a deep breath. Then he took a bite.

NOTIFICATION: WATER PARK FLYER

From

EVERYTHING YOU NEED TO KNOW ABOUT TOPSEA

by Fox & Coats

The Ice-Cream Man Returns

The ice-cream man hadn't come to Topsea for a long time. All the kids were depressed.

"I'm not even sure what ice cream tastes like anymore."

"You can still buy it at the supermarket, you know."

"It's not the same. My little sister doesn't even *like* Rocky Road unless there are actual rocks in it. . . ."

Then, late one night, there came a familiar jingle. Familiar—but a little unfamiliar, too.

Stranger. More haunting.

The music woke all the kids of Topsea, but none of the grown-ups. One by one, the kids climbed out of bed in their zombie

nightshirts and unicorn pajamas. Barefoot, they ran outside, heading for the irresistible tinkling sound.

Soon, every kid in town was running along the sidewalk, down Main Street, and toward the beach.

The music grew louder.

In a trance, the kids jogged along the shoreline. They climbed up the rocks, ignoring the yowling rock cats, and staggered onto the bluffs.

They stepped to the very edge. . . .

The music stopped.

All the kids looked at each other, dazed. Where were they? What had they done? Why were they all in their pajamas?

Suddenly dozens of anxious moms and terrified dads and grandparents and uncles and aunts and a chaos of older brothers and nannies and stepsisters who were home visiting from college came running up the bluffs, shouting the kids' names.

"Marisol! Oh dear, I *told* you you're afraid of heights. . . ."

"Olive! What were you thinking? You'll never make it to tomorrow's rehearsal if you fall off a cliff. . . ."

"Ahmed! Did you forget to put on your retainer *again*?"

In all the pandemonium, nobody heard the sound of screeching tires and a man's spooky cackling as he sped away in his truck.

Feeling confused and vaguely embarrassed, the kids stumbled their way back home and into their beds. The next morning, it seemed like a dream.

Except the bottoms of their feet were covered in sprinkles.

Jules

12.

Who Would Steal a Collection of Questions?

Jules was in a crabby mood.

Even the cafeteria workers' crab cupcakes couldn't cheer her up. In fact, they just reminded Jules that she was a failure.

Her crab investigation had hit a dead end. She knew deep in her gut that there was more to those crabs than met the eye . . . but she couldn't seem to prove it.

Which meant there was no story.

And if Jules was an investigative reporter without a story, then she was no investigative reporter at all. She might as well give up. Throw in the towel. Cease and desist. Cop out—

"Jules?"

A sad voice interrupted her thoughts. Jules pushed aside her half-finished crab cupcake as Quincy sat down across from her. His eyes were wide and shiny behind his glasses. "What's wrong?" Jules asked.

"Um . . ." Quincy swallowed. "It's my question collection. It's missing."

Jules whipped out her notepad and pen. "When did you see it last?" she asked briskly. "Who was with you? Where were you?"

Quincy's hands fidgeted. "Oh, those are such good questions. Um. Oh. Er. I don't know the answers!"

"It's okay," Jules reassured him. "We'll find your collection."

She tapped her pencil on her chin and thought hard. What would her stepsister do? Establish a motive, Jules told herself. So who would want to take a collection of questions?

Someone who had too many answers, of course!

"Come on!" Jules yanked Quincy's hand so hard his glasses slipped off his nose. He clutched them in his free hand as Jules dragged him to the counselor's office.

Mr. Zapple beamed at them. "Hello, Jules! Hello, Quincy! What brings you here?"

"Oh," Quincy said, replacing his glasses. "That's a very good question. I wish I could add it to my collection."

"Why can't you?" Mr. Zapple asked. "Where's your notebook?"

"Oh. Um. Er."

"It's gone," Jules announced. "Possibly stolen by someone who has all the answers. Like, say . . . a *school counselor*."

Mr. Zapple's eyes widened. "Me? I don't have Quincy's notebook!"

"Really?" Jules felt deflated. "Aw."

"And I don't have all the answers," Mr. Zapple added kindly. "In fact, I hardly have any. I just help students answer their own questions. You'd be surprised how often they realize they've been asking the wrong question all along!"

Jules considered this. "Do you think I'm asking the wrong question?"

"Perhaps," Mr. Zapple said. "Maybe the person who took Quincy's questions didn't take it because they have too many answers. Maybe they took it because they ask a lot of questions and their supply is running low."

"Hmm," Jules said. "So we're looking for someone who needs more questions. . . ."

Mr. Zapple smiled. "That sounds like a good place to start! Now, if you'll excuse me, I have story time with the kindergartners." He picked up a book. It had a picture of a troll lurking beneath a bridge on the cover.

Quincy's face lit up. "Oh, I remember that book! The troll makes everyone who wants to cross the bridge answer a question first. Most of the questions are really tricky. I collected all of them."

"Quincy, that's it!" Jules cried. "Trolls go through lots and lots of questions. Thanks, Mr. Zapple!"

She grabbed Quincy's hand and they raced out of the

office, out of the school, and all the way to the boardwalk.

"Mr. Troll? Mr. Troll!" Jules hopped and stomped on the boardwalk, stopping every few seconds to peer through the cracks. "Are you down there?"

"What a great question," Quincy said sadly. "I hope I can remember all of these."

"Don't worry," Jules told him. "We'll get your collection back soon enough."

She hoped she sounded confident. But the truth was, Jules wasn't so sure anymore. The troll wasn't answering. Maybe there *was* no troll. It's not like any of the kids had ever actually met him, other than Finn. And Jules wasn't sure that she'd heard Finn right, anyway.

Maybe this was just another false lead and Jules would never be as good of an investigative reporter as her stepsister. Jules stamped her foot in frustration.

Just then, a voice barked out from under them:

"HEY! Who's there?"

They stared down into a pair of beady eyes glinting through a crack in the boardwalk. Jules felt a flutter of nerves, but she ignored it.

"My name is Jules," she said. "I'm an investigative reporter. Or at least, I'm trying to be one. My friend Quincy's collection of questions has gone missing, possibly stolen. Do you have it?"

"Why would I have it?"

"Don't you ask everyone who crosses the boardwalk a question?"

"Why would I do that?"

Jules scratched her head. "Aren't you a troll?"

"What makes you think I'm a troll?"

"Argh!" Quincy cried suddenly, plugging his ears with his fingers. "So many wonderful questions!"

Jules glared down at the troll, hands on her hips. "Look, my friend is upset. Have you seen his collection or not?"

"Not," said the troll who wasn't a troll. "You kids lose all sorts of stuff when you go trip-trapping all over my roof, but I've never found a collection of questions. And when I do find anything, I return it."

"Oh. I'm really sorry." Jules sighed. Another dead end. "Maybe I'm still asking the wrong question, like Mr. Zapple said. Maybe the person who took Quincy's notebook didn't have all the answers, and maybe they weren't running low on questions."

"Those certainly aren't the only reasons someone might want a question collection. Anyone who's curious likes questions. My name's Billy, by the way. And it's *Ms.*, not *Mr.*"

"Curious." Jules thought hard. "Curious . . . oh! *Curious!* Thanks, Ms. Billy!"

She grabbed Quincy's hand once more. They ran toward the beach, panting as they came to a stop by the rocks.

The rocks were covered in all types of cats. There were tabby cats, calico cats, orange-striped cats, black cats. Some were tiny and fluffy, some were fat and silky. Their collective purr rumbled like a sleeping dragon.

Jules and Quincy stared at them. The cats stared back with curious eyes.

"I don't know why I didn't think of them first," Jules said to Quincy. "They did steal the milk from the cafeteria workers, after all."

The purring stopped. An indignant silence followed.

Jules took a deep breath. "We're looking for a collection of questions. And we think you have it. Cough it up, fur balls."

The rock cats looked at her. Then they looked at one another. Then they went back to purring and sunbathing.

Jules yowled in frustration. She turned to Quincy and started to ask him a question, but stopped when she saw his downcast expression.

She blinked. Maybe the problem wasn't that she'd been asking the wrong questions. Maybe the problem was that she'd been asking questions at all.

"Quincy," Jules said carefully. "Tell me the last question you wrote in your notebook."

Quincy's brow furrowed for a moment. Then he smiled.

"Cold enough for ya?"

Jules frowned. "But it's very warm outside."

"It is," Quincy agreed. "I was in the cafeteria having breakfast before school. The cafeteria workers were unloading a shipment of seaweed pops, and the freezer was wide open."

Jules beamed. "Let's go!"

They raced all the way back to the school, then burst through the doors of the kitchen. Nicky, who was scrubbing out the clam boiler, raised an eyebrow.

"You kids okay?"

"Please," Jules said, rubbing at a stitch in her side. "Breakfast . . . this morning . . ."

Nicky sighed. "Look, I'm sorry there wasn't any milk this morning. We were busy unloading a shipment of seaweed pops and didn't notice the PTA President sneaking in and replacing all the cheddar cheese with cheddar-flavored tofu. But tomorrow—"

Jules shook her head, still panting. "Not . . . cheese . . ."

"Notebook . . ." Quincy added between gulps of air. "Missing . . ."

"Oh, right!" Nicky smiled. "We found this after the lunch rush today, crammed inside the frozen yogurt machine. I suppose it's yours?"

She pulled Quincy's notebook from the pocket of her apron. It was a little damp and smelled like caramel-coconut swirl.

"My collection!" Quincy cried joyfully. "Thank you!" Clutching his notebook, he beamed at Jules. "And thank you for helping me find it. You're the best investigative reporter I know."

Jules stood up a little straighter. "Anytime," she said proudly. "I knew we'd figure it out eventually."

"Why are you so out of breath?" Nicky asked. "How many other places did you kids look?"

Quincy pulled out a pen and started scribbling away.

Jules grinned at Nicky. "Please hold your questions for now, ma'am. Quincy has enough to catch up on."

She flipped her notepad closed and stuck her pen behind her ear.

"And I have a crab investigation to get back to."

NEW STUDENT SURVEY (THIRD TRY)

by Davy Jones

1. Why did you move to Topsea?

~~My mom made me.~~

~~My mom got a new job at the seaweed cracker factory. I don't understand why people eat so much seaweed here.~~

My mom wanted a fresh start in a new town. I didn't understand why at first, but now I get it. And I think I might even like it here.

2. What are you most excited to learn about at Topsea School, and why?

~~I like math, because it makes sense. But the way Ms. Grimalkin teaches it is weird. She does multiplication tables by scratching them on the wall.~~

~~I liked our geography lesson, but it made me really hungry.~~

I like science so far. Bathymetry sounds really interesting! I think.

3. What's your biggest fear?

~~Getting attacked by those rock cats. They give me the creeps.~~

~~CRABS. And crab—they keep serving it in the cafeteria. The meat is practically black. But for some reason, everyone seems to love it.~~

Skeeball.

4. What is your favorite hobby?

~~Fishing.~~

~~Skeeball.~~

I'd like to learn how to paint!

5. What's your favorite flavor of ice cream?

~~Pistachio.~~

~~Jules told me she got bees in her ice cream once. So anything that doesn't have bees is fine with me.~~

. . . I can't remember.

6. Do you have any other thoughts you'd like to share?

Every day in Topsea is filled with surprises. WEIRD surprises! But mostly, they're the good kind of weird.

The kind my dad would have liked.

When I first moved here, thinking of my dad's reactions made me sad. Mostly because it reminded me of how much I miss him.

But lately, those thoughts make me smile, too.

Don't get me wrong! I still have a lot of questions about living in Topsea. (What's the prize for forty-five arcade tickets? Is Hanger Cliffs Water Park EVER going to open? WHAT IS THE DEAL WITH THOSE ROCK CATS?)

I'm starting to think I'll never get all the answers. . . .

But I'm also starting to feel okay with that.

NOTIFICATION: GRAVITY MAINTENANCE DAY

Courtesy of the Topsea Transportation and Flotation Authority

Topsea officials will be performing annual Gravity Maintenance next week in anticipation of the maybe-probably reopening of Hanger Cliffs Water Park. Residents are encouraged to stay indoors and follow these precautions:

1. Bolt your furniture to the floor. Lock all knickknacks and smaller appliances in a cupboard or closet.
2. Keep your windows CLOSED and LOCKED at all times.
3. If possible, take refuge in your basement. *However, NEVER enter your basement's basement during Gravity Maintenance.*
4. Helmets are not mandatory, but strongly encouraged.
5. Make sure to secure your pets before Gravity Maintenance begins!

Police will be on hot-air balloon patrol to assist any residents who find themselves airborne. If you see someone who needs assistance, do not attempt to rescue them. Remain indoors and call 555-SKY-SAVE to report the incident.

Quincy

13.

The Levitating Cake

Science was very important in Quincy's family. Hobbies were very important, too.

His mom studied botany and horticulture. That meant she was very good at gardening.

His other mom studied the physics of sound. That meant she was very good at playing the cello.

His little sister, Roxy, studied geology. That meant she had quite an impressive collection of pebbles for a two-year-old.

Like the rest of his family, Quincy loved science. But he didn't have a particular favorite field. There were just too many options! So he decided to collect questions. He could always worry about the answers later.

Quincy was very proud of his question collection, and he'd almost lost it. If it wasn't for Jules, his questions might still be trapped in the frozen yogurt machine. His parents had suggested he give Jules a gift to show his appreciation, and Quincy thought that was a great idea.

But the question was: What kind of gift?

"I guess I could make her a thank-you card," Quincy mused as he brought Roxy into the kitchen.

Although it was Saturday, Quincy's parents were doing important work in their basement's basement. They were too busy to help him come up with gift ideas. But Roxy was always willing to give her opinion. Quincy strapped her into her high chair and placed a handful of pebbles on her table.

"Gwabitty," Roxy said solemnly. She grabbed a pebble and started examining it. Quincy's little sister took geology very seriously.

"Hmm . . . or maybe I could paint her a picture."

"Meh," said Roxy.

Quincy sighed. "Yeah, that's more Runa's field." He tapped his fingers on the counter, thinking. Then his gaze fell on his mom's recipe wheel.

"I know!" Quincy exclaimed. "I'll bake something! Baked goods make excellent gifts, right?"

Roxy beamed and clapped. Quincy knew his parents would agree, too. After all, baking used lots of principles of chemistry and engineering and biology.

Quincy started flipping through his mom's recipe wheel. "Persimmon pudding, pickle pie, peppered pralines . . . oh, pound cake! Jules would like that, wouldn't she?"

Roxy shrieked happily, and a pebble fell out of her nostril. Quincy took that as a yes. He pulled out the recipe card and looked at all the instructions.

His hands started to sweat.

Quincy felt overwhelmed a lot. Like when he had to write a three-page research paper on the different types of world biomes. Or when he had to build a diorama based on a story about a book-loving girl who could make objects fly with her mind. Or when Ms. Grimalkin had asked him to help write a Bill of Rights for the classroom. Often, those types of projects sent Quincy into a little bit of a panic.

"If you ever feel overwhelmed, just stop and take a nice, deep breath!" his mom would say.

"Then remember to take every project one step at a time!" his other mom would add.

Usually, their advice helped. So Quincy took a nice, deep breath. Then he took the recipe step-by-step.

He assembled all the ingredients on the kitchen table: eggs, flour, sugar, milk, and a whole pound of butter. Then he gathered all the utensils his parents kept in the kitchen for extra-precise measurement: dropper pipettes and graduated cylinders and Erlenmeyer flasks.

Quincy preheated the oven. Then he started beating the butter to make it airy and extra creamy. The texture was almost perfect when he noticed the egg.

It was floating.

Only an inch or two off the table, but still.

Quincy let go of the stirring rod to push his glasses up his nose. Nervously, he watched the egg hover. What would his parents say if they were here? They would probably ask lots of questions. They would form a hypothesis about why an egg might float. Then they would test it to see if their theory was right.

Forming a hypothesis had always been difficult for Quincy. So many questions to answer! But he wanted to try.

"What would cause an egg to float?" he asked Roxy.

She spit a pebble on the floor, then shrugged.

Quincy's hands were sweating even more now. He started mixing sugar into the creamy butter—until a second egg rose off the table. Then a third. A fourth. Soon, all half-dozen eggs were bobbing peacefully over the flasks of milk.

"What would cause *all* the eggs to float?" he asked Roxy. But she was too busy shoving pebbles back into her mouth to respond.

Quincy set down the bowl and grabbed one of the floating eggs. When he cracked it against the side of the bowl, the yolk fell . . . up.

The bowl was rising, too. So was the stirring rod. So were Roxy's pebbles. So were the flasks of milk and the flour and the pipettes and cylinders and the bowl of fruit on the kitchen table.

So was *Quincy*!

He looked down at his own feet in surprise. "What might cause me to float?" he asked himself. "And the food? And the pebbles?"

"Oh. Um. Er," he replied unhelpfully.

This was too stressful. He needed a lab partner. And Quincy's lab partner was also his friend—maybe even his best friend. Quincy pushed himself off the counter, drifted over to the phone, and dialed.

"Hello?" came a slightly panicked voice.

"Hi, Dante," Quincy said. He was rising higher and higher off the floor. "I need help coming up with a hypothesis. I'm trying to bake a cake, and—"

"Quincy, I'm so glad you called!" Davy cried. "I'm floating! So's my bed! And—whoa, and my TV! What's going on?"

So many excellent questions! But Quincy had to focus on one. "Hmm. What would cause everything in town to float?"

He wiped his sweaty palms on his pants and looked around the kitchen. His eyes landed on a notice his parents had stuck on the refrigerator with magnets. And suddenly Quincy had a hypothesis he was quite positive was correct:

"Today is Gravity Maintenance Day!" he exclaimed. "Thanks, Dante. By the way, have you ever baked a cake in a no-gravity environment?"

"I'm tangled up in my ceiling fan," Davy said. "Why are you asking me about cake?"

"I'm baking one for Jules," Quincy explained. "I think I might have found a new hobby!"

"That's great!" Davy sounded like he was on the other end of a long tunnel. "I've never baked without gravity. Or done anything without gravity. Oh, there goes my fishing pole . . . and my swim trunks . . . and my—"

"Oh, that reminds me!" Quincy said excitedly. "Are you going to Hanger Cliffs Water Park tomorrow? It's finally reopening!"

Davy's voice was even more distant now. "What did you say? I dropped my phone! Uh-oh, it's floating toward my mom's aquarium, I hope it doesn't—"

There was a *SPLOOSH*, and then a dial tone.

Shrugging, Quincy hung up.

He couldn't believe he'd forgotten Gravity Maintenance Day. After all, that was why his parents were in their basement's basement. As scientists, they were part of the team performing maintenance. And much of the maintenance took place in the town's basements' basements.

Last night, Quincy had watched them bolt down the furniture in preparation. But he'd been so busy writing down questions like *Where did you put the hammer?* and *Did you remember to close the toilet lid?* and *Quincy, are you listening to us?* that he'd forgotten why his parents were securing everything in the first place.

"No gwabitty," he told Roxy, whose high chair was bolted safely to the floor.

She gave him a thumbs-up.

Quincy and his sister gazed around at the floating eggs and pebbles and flasks and fruit. Quincy decided he could still bake in a no-gravity situation. He just had to be careful.

He moonwalked over to the front hall closet to get his bike helmet. When he returned to the kitchen, the cake batter had begun rising out of the bowl. It looked like a sugary-buttery hand reaching for the ceiling.

Quincy's own hands shook a tiny bit. He told himself to stay calm. "One step at a time," he said.

First, Quincy flipped the bowl over to contain the batter. Next, he grabbed the flask of milk and held it under the bowl so that it flowed up. Just as he finished, something bright yellow smacked him in the forehead.

"Ow!" he cried.

He grabbed the airborne lemon. "This is Jules's favorite flavor of ice cream," he told Roxy. "Even though the ice-cream man always gives her storm-cloud sherbet—by accident, of course. Do you think she'd like lemon pound cake?"

Roxy didn't respond. Her cheeks bulged with pebbles.

"Well, I think she would."

Quincy floated over to the utensils drawer and—taking great care not to let the knives free—took out the cheese grater. Then he hovered beneath the bowl and started grating the lemon. The bright yellow zest wafted up into the batter. His hands finally stopped shaking. Baking was pretty relaxing.

Grinning, Quincy used the stirring rod to mix the batter before pouring it upside down into a round pan. But when he opened the oven, he hesitated.

"If I put the pan in the oven, the batter will float up to the top and burn," he thought out loud. "How can I keep the batter in the pan until it's finished baking?"

He needed to answer the question. Then he would have a hypothesis.

"*Nahgwaaah,*" Roxy suggested. Her mouth was still full, but Quincy knew what she meant.

"No gravity," he agreed. "So I need to bake this pound cake upside down."

Quincy floated on his side. He placed the pan upside down inside the oven. The bottom rested gently on the roof, containing the batter. He closed the oven door and smiled.

So long as Gravity Maintenance lasted for at least another hour, his cake would turn out just fine.

Quincy set the timer, then wrote his recipe on a card:

Lemon Pound Upside-Down Cake.
Bakes best in a no-gravity environment.

"Not a bad start for a new hobby," he said proudly. "The first original recipe in my collection!"

"Blarp!" Roxy bellowed in approval. Pebbles soared gracefully through the air like a stream of bubbles.

Quincy looked around the kitchen. The ceiling was covered in splotches of milk and splattered eggs. Flour and pebbles floated freely. At least the floor was spotless. He wondered if his parents would mind if he left cleanup for after Gravity Maintenance ended.

"Maybe when pigs fly," his mom would have said.

And if Quincy had looked out the kitchen window right at that moment, that's exactly what he would have seen.

THE TOPSEA SCHOOL GAZETTE

Today's Seaweed Level: Lingering and somewhat playful

ANSWER OF THE DAY
A palm tree!

FOUND: A book on the care and training of teacup pigs. Owner should contact Billy under the boardwalk.

PRINCIPAL'S PRINCIPLES

Hello, students! This is a friendly reminder that all students are encouraged to ask questions. Asking questions is a very important part of your education, and your teachers, counselors, and administrative staff are here to help you find answers.

On a separate note, Sunday's PTA meeting has been canceled. The weather's just too nice and warm for everyone to be cooped up inside—especially when Hanger Cliffs Water Park is finally reopening! I can't wait to grab a seaweed snow cone and try out the new rides—especially the Mermaid's Demise. Hope to see you there!

Your Pal,
Principal Josefina (Jo) King

EXPOSED: THE TRUTH ABOUT THE CRABS!

by Jules, Fifth-Grade Star Reporter

Since the arrival of the mysterious black crabs, this reporter has been stumped. The new crabs scared off the old crabs (still currently inhabiting the basement of Lost Soles; all sandals now half off!). The rock cats avoid them. They prefer living underground to living in the ocean. Folks, these crabs are simply not normal.

This reporter was just about ready to give up her search for the truth. Her head was spinning. But then she remembered her fortune card from Madam Flea and realized the answer had been in front of her all week. Solving the case was her destiny!

After luring a particularly large crab out from under the rocks, this reporter brought it to Talise's laboratory to test her hypothesis. And following extensive study in her laboratory, Talise verified what this reporter suspected: the crabs aren't actually crabs at all.

They're spiders.

Davy

14.

The Bottomless Cove

It was just another Sunday in Topsea, which meant Davy Jones was confused.

At long last, he'd decided to talk to his friends about his dad. Not all of his friends at once, of course—talking to them one-on-one would be a lot less intimidating. He'd climbed on his bike and started for Quincy's house, when:

"*Wheeeee!*"

Davy skidded to a stop as a kid ran past. Then four more. Then seven more. They were different ages, but had one thing in common: all of them were wearing bathing suits.

Was there a Wildcard Tide? Davy wondered. No, most of the kids were laughing, not screaming.

Feeling bewildered, he got back on his bike and rode a little farther.

"I've been waiting for this my whole life!"

Davy hit his brakes as three more kids ran by. They all wore swimsuits and inflatable floaties on their arms. A fourth girl trailed behind, probably because of the gigantic inner tube she was carrying.

"Hey!" Davy called. "Where are you all going?"

The girl stared at Davy like he'd grown a second head, maybe even a third one. "Hanger Cliffs Water Park opens today!" she exclaimed. "Didn't you get the notification in your locker?"

"Oh, right," Davy said. "I, um, forgot."

She snorted, then hurried to catch up with her friends. Davy watched her go, scratching his head.

The truth was, he hadn't gotten the notification. Because he still hadn't made it to his locker.

Every day before school—and sometimes after school, too—he cannonballed into the swimming pool. He swam deeper and deeper. But every single time, he had to come up for air before he reached the shimmering gray dot. It was a good thing Quincy didn't mind sharing his textbooks.

Davy watched another pair of kids sprint past, both of them wearing ruffled bikinis. He wondered if Quincy was already on his way to the water park. They'd talked on the phone just yesterday, during Gravity Maintenance. Why hadn't Quincy mentioned the park was reopening?

"Because he assumed I'd gotten the notification!" Davy said out loud.

For a moment, he felt better. Then he frowned.

"Wait—no, he wouldn't have," Davy said. "Quincy knows I've never made it to my locker. . . ."

Had his friends forgotten about him?

Davy was just starting to like living in Topsea. A big part of that was because he'd made such great friends. But none of them had remembered to tell him about Hanger Cliffs.

Then again, how could he expect them to remember him if they couldn't even remember his name?

"I like your jacket, Danzig."

"Hey, Dartanian, you've got a piece of seaweed in your ear."

"Are you sure you want to eat that, Draco?"

Davy sighed as another pack of kids ran by, all of them in swimsuits. He still didn't see any of his friends. They were probably already at the water park. Davy knew he could hurry home and put on his swimsuit, but the idea of showing up alone made him feel shy. The same way he'd felt on the first day of school.

Davy climbed back onto his bike and started to pedal away.

"Diego! Hey, Diego!"

This was getting ridiculous. For once, Davy decided not to pay any attention. But the call got more and more urgent.

"Diego! Please, I need your help!"

It was Nia. Davy turned his bike around with a sigh. He liked Nia, but by now he knew how dramatic she could be. Then he noticed she was wearing regular clothes, not a swimsuit.

"Why aren't you on your way to Hanger Cliffs?" he called.

Nia ran over to join him. Up close, he saw her eyes were red and puffy, and her usually neat braid was coming undone.

"Earl Grey's missing!" she cried.

Instantly, Davy felt bad about ignoring her. "Are you sure?"

Nia held up Earl Grey's leash. It was snapped in half. "Do you think somebody stole him?" she asked tearfully. "He's worth a lot of money—or at least, he was when I thought he was a teacup pig. I'm not sure what the market rate is for watch hogs nowadays."

Davy couldn't imagine anybody stealing Earl Grey. By now, he was larger than any kid in town—and most of the grown-ups, too. "When was the last time you saw him?"

"During Gravity Maintenance," Nia said. "I tied his leash beside his favorite mud hole so he wouldn't float away."

"Even if he did float away, he'd have landed by now, right?" Davy examined Earl Grey's leash. Up close, it didn't look snapped in half—it looked *gnawed* in half. "Those look like teeth marks. Maybe he escaped on his own?"

Nia shook her head. "Earl Grey would *never* leave me! I'll bet it was those horrible rock cats. They've held a grudge ever since he squealed on them about the stolen milk."

"Can cats hold grudges?" Davy asked.

"The rock cats sure can!"

Davy supposed he didn't doubt it. "Still, I don't know what the rock cats could do to a fully grown watch hog."

"I just have this feeling he's in trouble," Nia said. "Please help me find him, Diego!"

"It's not—" Davy sighed. "Of course I'll help."

Nia climbed onto the handlebars of Davy's bike. He pedaled back toward the school, dodging hollering packs of swimsuit-clad kids.

"Nia! Dennis!"

Davy braked as Quincy, Runa, and Jules ran toward them. Quincy wore turquoise swim trunks covered in tiny pineapples and a matching swim cap. Runa wore striped shorts, a floral tank top, and giant boat shoes. Jules's one-piece was black, white, and red all over. She was holding a giant yellow cake upside down. It was partially eaten.

"We've been looking everywhere for you guys!" she exclaimed with her mouth full.

"Really?" Davy said hopefully.

"We'd never go to Hanger Cliffs without our best friends!" Quincy beamed at Davy, who beamed back.

"Finn's going to meet us there," Runa said. "But where's Earl Grey?"

"He's *missing*," Nia said sadly. She showed them the leash and described what had happened.

"Nia, why didn't you ask me for help?" Jules's lower lip, which was covered in yellow frosting, quivered. "You know I'm an investigative reporter. And I've been getting so much better! Didn't you read my crab exposé?"

"Of course I did!" Nia sniffled. "Everybody knows you're the best investigator in Topsea. I was just . . . embarrassed. You're always telling me I need to take better care of Earl Grey."

"I think you take great care of Earl Grey! Now that you got the right training book." Jules beamed at Nia, who beamed back.

"All right, everyone!" Davy said. "We should split up. I'll head to the beach with . . ." He glanced at Runa and blushed. "With Nia. Quincy and Jules can search the school, and Runa can search the beach forest."

Runa's eyes lit up. "Ooh, I love the beach forest. This one time . . ." She stopped and shook her head. "I'll save it for later. Let's go!"

"You don't mind missing Hanger Cliffs?" Nia asked.

"Of course not," Quincy said. "I mean, of course we do, but Earl Grey is way more important."

Jules and Quincy ran off toward the school, Runa scampered toward the beach forest, and Nia and Davy rode toward the boardwalk. "Earl Grey!" they shouted, Davy's bike bouncing over the uneven planks.

CLANGCLANGCLANG.

Finn popped out from under the boardwalk, brandishing his square-shaped bell. He wore striped shorts, a floral tank top, and tiny boat shoes. "Can you keep it down, please?" he asked. "I was having some tea before heading to Hanger Cliffs, and sounds really echo down here—"

"Earl Grey is lost!" Nia cried. "Can you help us find him?"

Finn gasped. "Of course! Earl Grey is a good friend. He helped Runa save me when I got stuck to the chewing gum wall."

Davy blinked. "That really happened?"

He parked his bike, and the three kids searched the rocks, the beach, and the sand dunes. They didn't see Earl Grey anywhere. But they did find Talise down by the water, measuring a starfish with a complicated-looking tool. She wore a wet suit, goggles, and bright blue flippers.

"Oh, is Hanger Cliffs open yet?" she asked. "I got distracted—"

"Earl Grey is lost!" Nia cried.

Talise let go of the starfish. It cartwheeled over the sand before veering into the sea. "Did you check your basement's basement?"

Davy's eyes followed the prints the starfish had made. A few yards away, they crossed a trail of larger footprints.

"Hey," he said, pointing. "Aren't those hoofprints?"

"They *do* look like hoofprints!" Nia exclaimed. "Do you think they're watch-hog prints?"

Together, the kids followed the hoofprints across the beach. But before long, the hoofprints stopped right in the middle of the sand.

"I don't get it," Nia said.

"Look!" Davy pointed. "They begin again over there."

They hurried over. The hoofprints continued for a few more feet, then stopped again. "How peculiar," Talise said. "It almost appears as if the hog was leaping."

"Do watch hogs leap?" Finn wondered.

Nobody knew. They kept searching until they found the next set of hoofprints, closer to the water. Then more on the way to the boardwalk, and another set toward the bluffs. Davy hoped they wouldn't lead to the Untold Caves. He had a bad feeling about those caves.

The tracks didn't lead to the Untold Caves, though. They led through the beach forest, past a giant oak tree . . .

. . . and ended at the bottomless cove.

Runa, Jules, and Quincy joined them just as Nia burst into tears. "Earl Grey fell into the bottomless cove!" she sobbed. "We have to save him!"

All the kids leaned over the edge of the cove, peering in. Davy definitely didn't see any watch hogs. In fact, he couldn't see anything at all. The water was murky and dark. And cold-looking. *Really* cold-looking.

"How long can watch hogs hold their breath?" Quincy asked anxiously.

"A long time," Nia said. "I've been training Earl Grey for

the synchronized swim team. But he can't hold it forever—we need to hurry!"

"All right, listen up!" Jules said. "Someone needs to dive in to find him."

"Talise is the one with the diving license," Runa said.

Talise shook her head. "I'm sorry, I'm unable to. I'm recovering from a sinus infection. It's important not to dive when you have a sinus infection."

"Why?"

"Well, because your sinuses might burst. You see, the deeper a diver descends, the more the pressure builds up—"

"Hurry!" Nia exclaimed, jumping up and down.

"Dobby should go," Quincy suggested.

"Why me?" Davy said.

"Because of your locker, obviously! You're the second-most-experienced diver in Topsea."

"But I've never actually made it to my locker—"

Talise removed her goggles and handed them to Davy. "Unfortunately, my flippers are too small for you. Fortunately, it looks like you have abnormally large feet."

"Hey," Davy said.

"Just pretend you're at Hanger Cliffs," Jules said. "Rocketing down one of their sixteen exhilarating water slides, or floating down the lazy river right before the treacherous waterfall . . ."

Runa smiled encouragingly. "Don't worry. You'll be just fine!"

Davy didn't feel just fine. But Nia and Earl Grey needed him. He snapped on Talise's goggles, took a deep breath, and cannonballed into the bottomless cove.

The water was much colder than the school's swimming pool. And darker—Talise's goggles didn't help much at all. It was hard to tell which way was down. Or up. Davy was half afraid he'd swim the wrong way and end up in somebody's basement.

Something brushed Davy's hand. It didn't exactly *feel* like he thought a watch hog would feel, but he was running out of air. He grabbed it and lugged it toward the surface.

"Gahhh!" Davy gasped.

"A boot?" Runa said.

"Ooh, what size?" Finn asked.

"That's not Earl Grey," Nia said. "Hurry, Daven!"

Davy tossed the boot onto the shore. He took a big swallow of air and dived back down.

And down . . .

and down . . .

and down.

Could the bottomless cove really be bottomless? Davy wondered. Sure, "bottomless" was part of the name. But that could just be a figure of speech. More colorful than calling it "the incredibly deep cove that actually *does* have a bottom." Because there had to be a bottom somewhere. Right? If not, you'd swim right past the center of the earth. And then you'd be swimming up again.

The deeper Davy swam, the darker it got. He groped blindly

in the gloom. His fingers brushed against something else. It *really* didn't feel like a pig this time, but he grabbed it anyway and kicked toward the surface.

"Unhhh!" he gasped.

"Seaweed?" Runa said.

"That's not Earl Grey either," Nia said. "Hurry, Donald!"

It took a few tries to get the seaweed to detach itself from Davy's hand. Then he dove again.

And again. And again.

Each time, Davy swam deeper than the time before. He hauled up a bundle of rope. A moldy stuffed dog. A history textbook with all the pages missing. A teacup. A conch shell. Something small and rubbery, which felt less like a hog than ever, but Davy was getting tired.

"Ack, a rubber duck?" Runa said.

"Drat," Talise grumbled. "Of *course* it's a rubber duck."

"Are its painted eyes rubbed off?" Jules asked.

Davy blinked. "Huh?"

"You're supposed to put it in a bucket and freeze it. Didn't you get the notification in your locker?"

"I told you, I've never made it to my locker," Davy said.

"Hurry, Davina!" Nia exclaimed. "My heart is *breaking*!"

Davy took a deep breath.

SNORT!

Wait—that hadn't come out of his mouth. "Did anybody hear that?"

"Hear what?" Finn said.

"A snorting sound. I think it was coming from above us!"

Everybody looked up. Earl Grey gazed down at them from the giant oak tree where he was perched.

"Snort!" Earl Grey snorted. "Snort! Snort!"

"Earl Grey!" Nia shrieked in delight.

"He must have gotten stuck during Gravity Maintenance," Talise said. "No wonder his hoofprints were so far apart. He wasn't leaping from place to place. He was *floating*."

"How can we get him down?" Quincy asked.

Everybody looked at each other, then back up at Earl Grey. "He'll have to jump," Quincy said nervously. "Won't he? Oh dear."

Davy thought hard. Back home, he'd have called the police or the firefighters if a pet got stuck in a tree. But he wasn't back home. And anyway, "back home" wasn't Davy's home anymore—Topsea was home. Where coves could be bottomless. And sometimes, during Gravity Maintenance, even the best-trained watch hogs got stuck in trees.

Best trained. Suddenly Davy remembered Show-and-Tell, back when he'd first moved to town. "Hey, Nia!" he said. "Doesn't Earl Grey know how to jump through a hoop?"

She nodded. "But my hoop's at home. And it's too small for Earl Grey, anyway."

"What if we made a great big hoop with our arms?" Davy said.

Nia's face brightened. "Great idea!"

She grabbed Davy's hand. Davy grabbed Runa's hand. Runa grabbed Finn's hand. Finn grabbed Talise's hand. Talise grabbed Quincy's hand. Quincy grabbed Jules's hand. Jules grabbed Nia's other hand. Together, their arms made a perfect circle.

"Ready, Earl Grey?" Nia shouted.

"Snuffle," Earl Grey said resolutely.

"One, two, three . . . *Jump!*"

Earl Grey soared through the air, then landed daintily on all fours right in the very center of their encircled arms.

Nia laughed and hugged him, kissing his snout at least a dozen times. Then she hugged Davy, even though he was soaking wet. "You're a hero!" she exclaimed. "You saved Earl Grey!"

CLANGCLANGCLANG. "Three cheers for Davy!" Finn shouted, shaking his bell.

Davy blinked. "For *who*?"

Everybody cheered. "Davy! Davy! Davy! Davy!"

That was four cheers, but Davy didn't feel like correcting them. He stood there, dripping and beaming. Maybe it was silly, considering he hadn't saved Earl Grey on his own. Every single one of his friends had helped.

But for the first time since arriving in Topsea, he felt like he belonged.

"Hey, you guys!" Runa said. "It's not that late—want to see if we can still make it to Hanger Cliffs?"

Nia jumped up and down. "Yeah!"

Jules clapped her hands. "Let's go!"

Together, all seven kids ran toward Hanger Cliffs, Earl Grey trotting loyally behind them. As they drew closer, Davy expected to hear splashing and joyful shrieking.

But the water park was . . . *silent.*

A great big padlock hung on the iron gate. Above it, somebody had taped a notification:

HANGER CLIFFS WATER PARK
Nail-biting, edge-of-your seat fun!

The park is currently
~~Open~~ Closed*

The park will resume
operation on . . . .?

* *due to sudden "crab" infestation*

"*'Crab'* infestation?" Nia read unhappily.

"I guess it makes sense," Talise said. "Considering they're not actually crabs, they're—"

"I don't want to talk about it!" Davy shuddered.

The kids all laughed. "No problem, Davy," Jules said.

Davy couldn't help smiling at the sound of his name. And then, all of a sudden, he blurted out: "But there *is* something I'd really like to talk to you guys about, though. *Someone*, actually. Someone who was really important to me."

Quincy smiled. "Of course!"

"We'd be happy to listen," Finn agreed. Earl Grey nodded.

"Right now?" Davy asked.

"Sure!" Runa nodded. "There's no better time for a good story."

Davy hesitated, looking at his friends. All of them at once. He felt a little intimidated, but not as much as he'd thought.

Finally, he shrugged. "Why not?"

* * *

The next day at school, Davy was determined to make it to his locker.

He snapped on Talise's goggles and headed straight for the swimming pool. In the shallow end, the kindergarten class was playing dog tag. "AROOOO!" they howled, taking turns being swept out to sea.

Davy climbed atop the diving board. The pool was still very, very deep. But nowhere as deep as the bottomless cove. In fact, he could see the bottom from where he stood.

But he couldn't see his locker anywhere.

That was strange. He sucked in a huge breath and cannonballed into the pool anyway. He searched and searched, but his locker was nowhere to be found.

Davy stopped by the guidance counselor's office just as the tardy bell rang. "Good morning, Mr. Zapple," he said.

"Good morning!" Mr. Zapple set down his copy of the school newspaper. For a moment, Davy caught a glimpse of the headline:

HANGER CLIFFS SABOTAGE
PTA Prez Busted

"I've finished my survey," Davy said. "I'm sorry for all the cross-outs. It took me a while to figure things out."

"That's normal," Mr. Zapple said, accepting Davy's survey. "Did you get a chance to read *Everything You Need to Know About Topsea?*"

"Wait," Davy said. "*Everything You Need to Know About Topsea* is a *book?*"

Mr. Zapple nodded. "It should have been in your locker."

"That would have been helpful!" Davy sighed. "I never made it to my locker. I searched the entire pool."

"Oh, that's why you're wet! I'm sorry, I forgot to tell you—we had to move your locker."

"You did?"

Mr. Zapple nodded. "The synchronized swim team said it was getting in the way of their sea-serpent formation. Now it's on top of the school."

Davy blinked several times. "But why . . . how do I . . ."

"You'll be just fine," Mr. Zapple told him. "Good luck, Davy!" He waved as Davy left the office. This time, Davy waved back.

He knew he'd be just fine.

To whoever finds this letter:

Perhaps you think you know everything you need to know about Topsea. However, you most likely do not. (Even if you've read *Everything You Need to Know About Topsea* cover to cover.)

You did not, for example, know that a bottle containing a message was waiting for you as you were collecting clamshells or studying tide pools or measuring the ocean depth with a sounding line.

You probably do not know what the lighthouse keeper is up to right now. Or why a toothy, rock-loving creature is currently watching you read this. And you definitely do NOT know what's hidden in the Untold Caves.

You may not know everything about Topsea. But thanks to this letter, you now know this: something BIG is coming.

VERY big.

Keep your eye on the tides,

Fox & Coats

Acknowledgments

Our incredible editors, Emily Meehan and Hannah Allaman, designer Maria Elias, and the rest of the Disney Hyperion team.

Rachel Sanson, illustrator of our dreams (even the spooky ones).

Our brilliant agents, Jaida Temperly and Sarah Davies, along with the teams at New Leaf Literary & Media and Greenhouse Literary Agency. Seaweed cookies for all.

Our families and friends, especially Alison Cherry, Sarah Enni, Kate Hart, Kaitlin Ward, Maurene Goo, Alex Kahler, Lindsay Ribar, Rebecca Behrens, Claire Legrand, and Josh Schusterman. They never fear what we find in our basements—well, except for that one thing.

Teddy Fox and Adi, our ~~canine~~ mythological mascots. The rock cats also insist on being acknowledged, even though they probably did more harm than good.

Hey, what's that scratching sound?

Turn the page for a sneak peek at the sequel to

A Friendly Town That's Almost Always by the Ocean!

From

EVERYTHING ELSE YOU NEED TO KNOW ABOUT TOPSEΛ

by Fox & Coats

The Endless Pier

There is only one pier in the town of Topsea.

There are also quite a few docks. A boardwalk that would make a great racetrack, if you don't mind a troll shouting at you. But there is only one pier.

Fortunately, it's endless.

"Endless?" you might ask. "How can a pier be *endless*? Even the Endless Nachos at Nico's Taqueria end when he runs out of seaweed chips."

Good point. To figure it out, we should probably start at the beginning.

The beginning of the endless pier, we mean. It starts right here, on Topsea's beaches. Let's walk along it, shall we?

(Oops! Watch out for that broken plank!)

Everything has a beginning. And an ending, too. Like this book you're holding. There's a first page and a last page, right? Unless the rock cats got to it—they really like spoiling the endings of things.

If everything has an ending, that means this pier does, too.

But where? A little math might help. If the pier is twice as long as we've walked, that means we're halfway. Should we keep going? Or should we turn back?

(Look at those bubbles in the water. . . . Never mind, they're gone.)

How long *have* we been walking?

It feels like forever. But that can't be true. We know we started on Topsea's beaches, even if we can't see them from here. Before we saw the bubbles. Before the broken plank. We started at the beginning. Right?

Do we know for sure?

Maybe the pier *ends* on Topsea's beaches.

Maybe we started at the ending without realizing it.

And maybe, wherever the pier actually begins, somebody—or something—is walking toward us, too.

In the town of Topsea, there is only one.

Talise

Story 1:

SHLORPP!!!

SQUEAK!

"Drat," Talise muttered.

Quickly, she yanked her hand from her backpack and zipped it shut. She hoped nobody else in Ms. Grimalkin's fifth-grade class had heard the telltale sound.

"Was that a rubber duck?" Runa asked, leaning across the aisle. She had black hair cut into angles. Her cheeks had paint on them.

Talise was no good at lying. "Quite possibly," she said with a sigh.

"Rubber ducks are dangerous!" Jules exclaimed, leaning

across the other aisle. She had blond hair curled into spirals. Her cheeks had freckles on them.

"Not necessarily," Talise said. "They're only dangerous if they have eyes. I avoided looking inside my backpack just in case."

"Is anything the matter?" Ms. Grimalkin asked.

"Talise has a rubber duck in her backpack," Jules told their teacher.

Now everyone in class was staring. Talise started to feel upset on the inside. She disliked people staring at her. Possibly even more than rubber ducks.

And she *really* disliked rubber ducks!

Rubber ducks with rubbed-off eyes seemed to pop up everywhere Talise went. She found them stuffed in her bag of scuba gear. Hiding in her clam chowder. Bobbing in her extra-deep soaking bathtub. Once, she'd heard a knock at the door and opened it to find rubbed-off eyes gazing at her from the front porch.

Ms. Grimalkin walked over to Talise's desk. "Do you have a rubber duck in your backpack, Talise?" she asked.

"I may or may not." It wasn't a lie, because Talise hadn't actually *seen* the rubber duck.

"That doesn't make sense," Jules protested.

"Sure it does," Runa said helpfully. "If you think about it, *everybody's* backpacks may or may not have rubber ducks in them."

Quincy gasped so hard his glasses fell off. "Oh dear!"

Davy scratched his head. "Wait—both can't be true at the same time."

"Unless *neither* is!" Nia said dramatically.

"Nobody can be sure until they check," Finn added in a diplomatic manner.

Ms. Grimalkin massaged her temples. "That's enough, everyone. Talise, would you please unzip your backpack?"

Talise unzipped her backpack. A rubber duck stared back at her. It didn't have any eyes, but her classmates still recoiled.

"Drat," Talise said. She disliked rubber ducks staring at her most of all.

While the other kids went to recess, Talise joined Ms. Grimalkin at her desk. She had stripy-looking gray hair and extremely sharp nails. But behind her tortoiseshell glasses, her eyes were kind. "Why did you bring a rubber duck to school, Talise?" she asked.

"I thought it was my sea blob," Talise replied.

"Your *sea blob*?"

"Not a live sea blob, an inanimate one. Made of foam. Clara gave it to me." Clara was Talise's therapist. They met once a week and talked about all kinds of things. She had told Talise to squeeze the sea blob anytime she felt anxious. "I was very tired this morning. I must have grabbed a rubber duck instead."

"I'm glad your sessions with Clara have been helpful," Ms. Grimalkin said. "But why were you tired this morning?"

"Because of the ocean."

"The ocean?"

"I was working on my math homework," Talise explained. "Then I started thinking about how two-thirds of the earth's surface is ocean. And how ninety-five percent of the ocean is still undiscovered. You see, there's the deep sea, and the *deep*-deep sea, and the even deeper sea than that—"

"Did you finish your math homework?" Ms. Grimalkin interrupted.

"I did not," Talise said.

"Well, thank you for being truthful."

"You're welcome."

Ms. Grimalkin drummed her pointy fingernails on her desk. "How about this. If you spend the rest of recess finishing your homework, I'll take the whole class to the beach this afternoon! What do you think?"

Talise nodded politely. "I feel very thrilled, thank you."

* * *

First, Talise pulled on her wet suit, flippers, and mask. Next, she strapped on her air tank, weight belt, and buoyancy vest. Last of all, she grabbed her depth gauge, underwater compass, and logbook: the waterproof notepad she used to log her dives.

She popped her regulator into her mouth. Then she flip-flipped over the sand to the rest of the class.

"Blurp blop bloop," she said.

"Talise," Ms. Grimalkin said. "We're only beachcombing today. If you'd needed diving equipment, I would have told you."

Talise glanced at her classmates, who were staring at her again. Even though the big blue ocean was *right there* beside them, they all wore land clothes. (Except for Nia's watch hog, Earl Grey. He didn't wear any clothes—unless you counted the teacup Nia had tied to his tail with a purple ribbon.)

"Blaaaaaargh," Talise sighed into her regulator.

There were many things Talise understood long before her classmates did. Like when Seaweed Season was approaching. (In approximately thirty-four days.)

Or what next Saturday's tide might be. (Severely Low with a threat of Wildcard.)

Or how to identify every tooth that washed up on Topsea's beaches. (Even before the Town Committee for Dental and Coastal Hygiene released its annual guide.)

As Topsea's only bathymetrist, Talise had studied the ocean more than anyone in Topsea. And now that she had a deep-sea-diving license, she didn't need to wait for a Vanishing Tide to explore it!

Her classmates found that very impressive.

But they understood many other things long before Talise did. Like when a wet suit was appropriate. (Talise would wear hers every day if she could.)

Or the difference between telling a story and lying.

Or each other. Talise's classmates understood each other immediately. But it took Talise a little extra effort.

"Sometimes, it's like they speak another language," Talise had complained to Clara during one therapy session. "Or lots of different ones."

"More like different dialects," Clara had suggested.

"What are dialects?"

"Dialects are different ways of speaking the same language," Clara had explained. "For example, Spanish is spoken differently in Mexico and Puerto Rico, where I'm from. Or Chile and Honduras.

Even in different parts of Spain! Once you've figured out your classmates' dialects, perhaps you'll understand them more easily."

Talise had liked that. "Do blue whales use different dialects in different parts of the ocean?"

Clara had smiled. "They probably do."

Once she had put on her land clothes, Talise rejoined the rest of the class. Ms. Grimalkin was handing out buckets and beachcombs.

"Collect anything odd or exceptional that you find," the teacher said. "According to the Town Committee for Tideland and Bath Toy Safety, even more peculiar items have been washing ashore lately."

"Oh, how *mysterious*!" Nia hopped up and down. So did her long, brown braid. Earl Grey tried to hop, but his hooves never left the ground.

"There is probably a logical explanation," Talise said.

"What's the fun in *that*?"

Nia's dialect was Ecstatic/Dramatic. One time, Talise's mother had arranged for Talise to play at Nia's house, and they'd spent the afternoon watching Mexican soap operas with Nia's nanny. All the characters were very dramatic. Talise understood Nia's dialect a bit more after that.

"Everybody, partner up!" Ms. Grimalkin said. "I'm off to find some lunch."

As usual, the best friends reached for their best friends. Finn reached for Runa's hand. Nia reached for Jules's hand. Davy reached for Quincy's hand. Talise reached for her sea blob, then remembered she'd left it at home.

Oh dear," Quincy said. "You don't have a partner *again*?"

Quincy's dialect was Considerate/Overwhelmed. He was probably the kindest kid Talise knew. He always thought about others—so much it occasionally made him anxious. That was a feeling Talise understood extremely well.

"I don't mind working alone," she told him. It was true. (Even if she had to remind herself sometimes.)

"She'll be fine," Nia said. "Talise knows more about the ocean than any kid in Topsea!"

"I know more about the ocean than any grown-up in Topsea, too," Talise said.

Jules raised her eyebrows. "Is that a fact?"

Jules's dialect was Clever/Overbearing. As the fifth grade's star reporter of the *Topsea Gazette*, she could get to the bottom of any mystery. Talise appreciated her attention to detail. Although sometimes Jules cared so much about being factual she clashed with her classmates.

"Because bathymetrists mainly study the bottom of the ocean, right?" Jules continued. "The lighthouse keeper proba-bly knows more about the top—"

"Where is the lighthouse keeper, anyway?" Runa asked.

As the other kids turned to look at the lighthouse, Talise walked away. She glanced back once, but nobody seemed to notice she'd left.

"I don't mind working alone," she reminded herself.

It was better that way. Talise's classmates didn't really share her interests—and Ms. Grimalkin usually gave her extra credit, which she liked.

And as long as she had the ocean, she was never *truly* alone.

Talise walked along the shoreline. Currently, it was Low Tide verging on Severely Low, so there was a lot to see. Tide pools bustled with activity. Gulls and plovers pecked for meals. The air was approximately 67 degrees Fahrenheit, while the ocean was closer to 59 degrees. It would be even colder at the bottom, but that's what a wet suit was for.

"I bet I'd find tons of peculiar items on the ocean floor," Talise said.

But the assignment was beachcombing, not seacombing, so she began to search the sand. All she found was a flamingo tongue, a kitten's paw, and a handful of baby ears.

"Just a bunch of common shells," she sighed.

After a while, Davy and Quincy caught up with Talise. "Look what I found!" Davy said, his eyes bright. "Do you think it's a *fang*?"

Davy's dialect was Eager/Brave. He was the newest kid in Ms. Grimalkin's class. Everybody liked him, including Talise— even though he already seemed to understand Topsea's dialects better than she did.

"Indeed," Talise replied. "Do either of you have a toothbrush?"

"Why would I—" Davy began.

"Of course!" Quincy interrupted, pulling one from his pocket.

Talise used it to scrub dirt off the fang's nonpointy end. "I'm trying to determine if it has been broken off or snapped off," she explained.

Davy blink-blinked. "What's the difference?"

"Snapped-off fangs are mostly useless."

"Uh, I understand," Davy said. But his brow was furrowed, which usually meant a person didn't understand. So was he lying?

Talise was about to ask—but then she noticed an odd collection of bubbles at the water's edge, near Finn and Runa. She hurried over, then crouched down to check if any of them were rubber-duck eyes.

No eyes, only bubbles. Talise smiled.

When she stood up, Runa and Finn were smiling, too. "It's nice to see you in a good mood!" Finn exclaimed in his tiny voice.

"I am usually in a good mood," Talise said. "It just doesn't always show on the outside."

"Like the lighthouse keeper," Finn joked.

Finn's dialect was Friendly/Mouse. He was very polite, but also made funny jokes sometimes. At least, the other kids laughed. (When they managed to hear him.) Jokes weren't always logical, and sometimes it took Talise a little extra effort to figure out *why* they were funny.

"The lighthouse keeper does go outside the lighthouse!" Runa said. "One time, I saw her dive into the ocean and start swimming. She just kept swimming and swimming—even past the end of the endless pier. . . ."

Talise still hadn't figured out Runa's dialect.

That was because Talise rarely knew when she was telling the truth, and when she was making something up. Runa painted, too. Her paintings made even less sense than her stories. But then, Talise never really saw the point of art in the first place.

Sometimes, asking a question helped Talise figure out the truth. "Did the lighthouse keeper have the appropriate diving gear?" she asked.

Other times, it backfired. "Even I didn't believe that one!" Finn said, giggling. "The pier *has* no end."

Talise felt embarrassed on the inside. It made her want to jump into the ocean and keep swimming, just like the lighthouse keeper. Not just out to sea, but *into* sea. The deeper, the better. All the most interesting things were below the surface.

If Talise had the choice, she'd live in the ocean forever and ever.

She glanced away—and noticed the odd bubbles again. Even if none were rubber-duck eyes, she had a funny feeling about them.

Was there something interesting below the surface?

Talise flexed her fingers, then jammed her hand into the sand. At first, all she felt was a squishy, mucky sensation. It was quite pleasant. Then she touched something hard. She wiggled her fingers until they were wrapped around it. Using all her strength, she pulled it out.

SHLORPP!!!

The sound was so loud all her classmates came running.

"Is that a bottle?" Finn asked.

It was a bottle. More specifically, a barnacle-covered bottle with a salt-crusted cork jammed in one end. Talise pried it out—*POP*. Then she peered inside, keeping a safe distance from the mouth of the bottle, in case a crab tried to pinch her eyeball. It had happened before.

"Is there something inside?" Quincy asked.

There was something inside. Talise shook a small, rolled-up piece of paper into her hand. When she looked more closely, she saw it wasn't actually paper—it was a very thin piece of tree bark.

"Does it have writing on it?" Jules asked.

It had writing on it. All the kids leaned in to read except Nia, who jumped up and down exclaiming, "What does it *say*? What does it *say*?"

The kids all stared at each other.

"Hull . . ." Runa read. "Maybe they're just saying hullo?"

"Hullo?" Finn repeated.

"It's how they say hello in Great Britain."

"But look at the first letters," Quincy said, sounding worried. "They spell out HELP!"

Nia clapped her hands over her mouth. "Maybe somebody's stranded on a desert island! That happened in one of Nanny's telenovelas."

"You mean a *deserted* island," Jules said.

"That's what I said!"

"No, you said '*desert*.' 'Deserted' means there's nobody there. Is there even such a thing as a desert island?"

"Certainly," Talise said. "Some islands contain deserts. Of course, it depends on what hemisphere the island is located in, and also the size of the island. The larger the island, the more likely—"

"So somebody's stranded on some kind of island," Davy said. "Maybe."

"That bottle is *ancient*!" Jules said. "It's not trying to tell us anything at all."

At last, Ms. Grimalkin joined them. "What an interesting find!" she said, picking her teeth with a very fine fishbone. "Talise, I'm giving you ten points extra credit for your determination."

Talise kept staring at the note.

An extremely strong feeling rose in her chest. Like her very own personal tide. She didn't know if the message had come from a deserted island. Or a desert island. Or a deserted desert island. Or anybody at all.

But it *had* come from the ocean.

The ocean had sent Talise a message.

It took a little extra effort to translate, but she thought she understood. She didn't know whether it was logical, but for once, she didn't care.

"The ocean wants me to build a boat," Talise said.

Everybody stared at her like she spoke a different language.

TALISE'S LOGBOOK

Name: Talise Villepreux
Date: Friday
Location: Topsea beach
Time in: 2:00 **Time out:** 3:00 **Bottom Time:** None
Depth: Extremely Shallow
Temperature: Warm
Visibility: Slightly foggy

Observations:

My apologies, Logbook: beachcombing is not a form of diving. But today, I found it almost as exciting as a dive. I found a message in a bottle!

It appears to be a boat schematic, or a simple sketch that shows you how something is built. I have identified four words:

1. Hull
2. Engine
3. Luff
4. Propeller

The bottle is obviously quite old. There must be a reason the ocean decided to send it to shore *NOW*. I believe the ocean wants me to build a boat.

Do you think that is silly, Logbook? My classmates seem to. But they spend all their free time with their best friends. I spend all my free time with the ocean. Therefore, I am the kid most likely to translate the ocean's dialect. (With a little help from the library, of course.)

Building a boat alone will be a challenge. I suppose it's a good thing I'm used to working without a buddy. In fact, I would prefer to take on this endeavor alone.

Really.